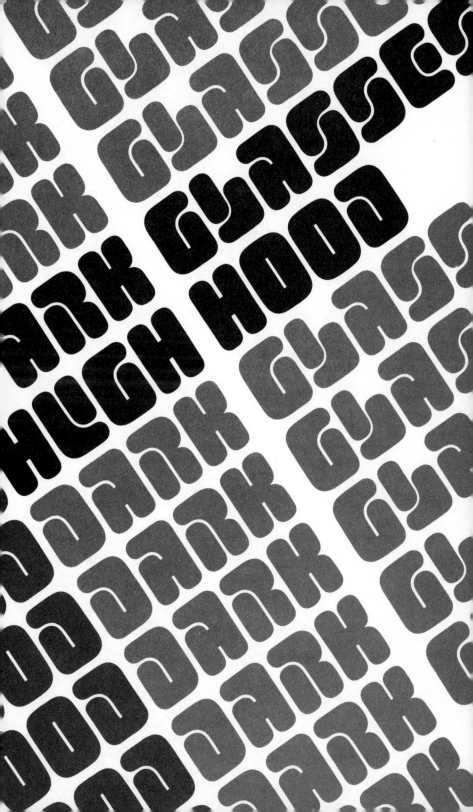

ISBN 0 88750 208 3 (hardcover)
ISBN 0 88750 209 1 (softcover)

Editor: Gail Low. Design: Michael Macklem

Printed in Canada

PUBLISHED IN CANADA BY OBERON PRESS

For now we see through a glass darkly; but then face to face
—I Cor. 13. xii.

CONTENTS

ALSO BY HUGH HOOD

Novels

White Figure, White Ground
The Camera Always Lies
A Game of Touch
You Cant Get There From Here
The New Age/Le nouveau siècle
   I: The Swing in the Garden

Stories

Flying a Red Kite
Around the Mountain: Scenes from Montréal Life
The Fruit Man, the Meat Man & the Manager

Non-Fiction

Strength Down Centre: the Jean Béliveau Story
The Governor's Bridge is Closed

This book is for my friend, Sam Tata.

Going Out as a Ghost

The children were preparing for Halloween, a festival they preferred to Christmas. The sombre mysterious end of October, when it grows colder and nobody yet knows how cold it may become, had always seemed more inviting to them than the steady weather of the solstice. They set great store by their costumes—had in different years presented themselves as Laurel and Hardy, four Marx brothers, knights in armour and hairy serfs, the two ends of a horse. They were a quartet agreeably near in age inclined to form pairs, liking to complement one another: master and slave, fat man and thin.

Their father, a confused man, joked with them about the reach and complication of these conceptions. "Going to go out this year?" he would inquire as they grew older. "What are you going out as?" The boys would argue between themselves, the girls exchange secret smiles, giving nothing away.

"I'll throw a sheet over my head and cut holes in it," their father would say at the very last minute. "I'm going out as a ghost." And the entire family would laugh uproariously, for this struck them as the lowest deep of impoverished fantasy. "Going out as a ghost," they all sang together, laughing, but inwardly troubled by the concept of dressing up as a clown or a cowboy. Such children could—probably did—miss altogether the intense, absorbed September and October during which the dress-up box was emptied, filled, emptied: old organdy and silk from costumes of years past held to the light. They had also a property box filled with daggers, stilettos, swords, false noses, wigs, grotesque false ears. Theatrical make-up was available, nose putty, crêpe hair. A family half sunk in show-business. All this began in late summer with vacation still in progress.

"If you're going into town, bring back my gorilla mask," said the older of the boys to his father on a Wednesday in late August. "I want to compare the fur."

"Where is it in the house? In your closet?"

"It's hanging on the light fixture in our room," said the younger boy. "I hung it there to make it look like a head sticking out of the wall."

"There should be a gorilla's hind-end sticking out of the wall in the next bedroom," said the father. He chatted amusingly with the children, but the image of the gorilla mask stayed with him disagreeably as he drove into the city. One of those rubber, over-the-head, monster disguises which can be found at theatrical costumers, it had been a birthday gift to his son, who had a collection of them: Dracula, Frankenstein's monster, the Wolf-Man, the Gorilla. In a poor light the thing was genuinely horrific and might prove shocking to house-holders on that dreary night nine weeks in the future. He was troubled by the human cast of the bestial shape. The coarse red of the cheeks, upturned snout, matted dangling hair, the powdery texture of the pliant rubbery skin. The boys played up certain simian characteristics in their movements; they liked to lower their hands around their knees by flexing the knee-joints. They would gibber in simulated ape-language. The younger boy often hung head downward in trees. With the gorilla mask over either head, full disguise was at once effected, a whole transformation of behaviour threatened. "Now I'm going to tear you limb from limb," they would say.

He had further worries, minor repairs impending on his automobile, which gave trouble as he drove along; the radiator leaked, spreading the odour of coolant through the passenger compartment, the smell of ethylene glycol, and some sweetish, doubtless wholly poisonous, additive—radiator cleanser or

8

sealer; there might be holes in the hoses. Late in the day he arrived in his city neighbourhood and left the auto with a local service man who at once, before his eyes, dismantled it, rendering it inoperative. "Tomorrow, one o'clock," said the mechanic, a highly trustworthy man.

"Going back to the country in the afternoon."

"You can have it by one. Not before."

He was glad to leave his car sitting on the lot, always felt better about it at such times, as one does about the seriously-ill member of the family who is at last "in good hands." As he walked the short distance to his empty house, it began to rain, then in the next hour settled into a steady downpour. He let himself in, stepped over the pile of mail lying on the floor below the letter slot, into the quiet hall. He had always liked the look of this house in the late afternoon with no electric light on; what light there was entered freely through large windows front and rear, then diffused itself into the corners of dark halls. He mounted to the second floor and standing in the doorway of his sons' bedroom he saw the gorilla mask hanging over the light socket, from which the bulb had been removed. Outside the rain continued to fall; it was now very dark for this time of year. The house was shut tight and stuffy, yet the mask moved and lifted slightly in some faint air current. He stared. He decided to have his evening meal delivered, Chinese, or barbecued chicken, no need to go out again. He might call a friend, see if he wanted to watch a late movie. What else had the kids asked for, was it masking tape?

Later he shuffled through the mail, discarded almost all, phoned for chicken, phoned David, who agreed to drive round at 9.30. Unmarried, self-employed, chronically at loose ends at night, David seemed pleased to be asked. "There are two good films on tonight," he said. "I hope my car starts." He came a little early, barely past nine, surprising his host, who was ensconced before the TV in the basement, picking chicken from the spaces between his teeth, listening to the rain, not

9

making much sense of the program he watched, which was loud. The doorbell rang several times before he grasped that it was not part of the soundtrack, which might well have had bells in it.

He switched on the porch light and peered out at the rain. Might as well be Halloween, he thought, and opened the door for David. "You're early."

"You said any time. You're alone, right? How much do you charge to haunt a house anyway?"

"What makes you say that?"

"I just thought of it. Your house is always a little haunted, you know." This seemed a disobliging comment which he could only ignore; they descended to the TV which they watched with pleasure for over an hour, until the telephone rang. This bell, different in tone from the doorbell, could not be assimilated to the sound of TV, had to be answered at once or attention would stray. He climbed unwillingly to the ground floor and went to the telephone in the studio at the very back of the house, where he fondled the clamorous instrument, gazing through the huge window at shining wetness. He put the receiver to his ear.

"Bet you don't know who this is," said a melodious voice. The line clicked and crackled strangely; the voice echoed, seemed familiar, then wholly unrecognizable. He had heard it, he knew, but how very long ago. "Bet you don't know who this is. . . this is. . . is. . . who?"

"We were in school together," he said firmly, shutting off the unsteady echoes.

The voice cooed, "You're getting close."

He listened harder; he had heard the voice somewhere in the past. There was a *castrato* music to it, high, sexually elastic though certainly male. "It's Philly White."

"Who?"

"Philly White. We went to parish school together, don't you remember the Whites, my brother Bob, my sister Pauline?

We made our First Holy Communion together."

"So we did. So we did. Of course I remember. You had smallpox when we were in, the third grade?"

He could remember the effects of the disease vividly, the spoiled face, the depth of indentation of the small round scars, about the size of a flake of confetti. His complexion had been like his name, white, the holes in his face changing colour as embarrassment or exposure moved the boy. He had often been in trouble with the teachers, hadn't been heard from in forty years. The voice was irrefutable testimony, when linked to a past and a name.

"I'm here at the Prevention Centre on Parthenais Street." The voice in the receiver pronounced the name wrong, as an Ontarian would, and translated the name of the institution too literally. *Centre de Prevention* doesn't mean "prevention centre," it means "detention centre," a quasi-jail where persons are held to await trial or, in certain cases, sentencing after conviction. Until now he had never heard of the place or seen it, knew nothing about it, couldn't have identified it from glimpses at a distance. It is a deceptive building. It is the embodiment of a lie. It doesn't look like what it is; suicide is routine inside. Men have spent fifteen months there awaiting trial, the presumed innocent often treated far worse than the proven guilty —because the innocence is purely formal and presumptive. Most inmates are habitual offenders. None of this was familiar to him. "What are they holding you for?" he asked.

"Some trouble about a cheque. Well, actually two cheques. Three. You knew my family, you knew Bob was ordained, you knew. . . I was married there for a while; then I moved out west. I had a car business in Vancouver and then came back east. Two little girls. We're separated now of course. . . you're the only one here in the city. . . I don't want my wife to know yet. I was hoping for a reconciliation. I want to get straightened out and start again."

"What's the charge?" He felt proud of the way he phrased

11

the question; he had no contact with police, courts, criminals, or even people who were being held, detained, prevented. "Have they got anything to go on?"

"Actually. . ." indecision floated into the quavering voice. "I can't talk any more; they're taking me back. They might let you see me. Could you try to see me?"

"The charge?"

"Matter of two years. . . I've been sentenced. . ." He never found out whether the term of the sentence was two years, or whether a longer term might be reduced to two for good conduct. "They're deciding whether to send me to a dry-out clinic. There's a problem of alcoholism. And they're waiting for information from Vancouver."

"What sort of information?" He felt damp; the studio was damp.

". . . conviction for fraud. . . not serious."

"What else?"

"Hotel bills in Dorval. They brought me in from Dorval. I was there a month. I have to go now." It sounded as if the call had been cut off at the main switchboard. He put the receiver into its cradle and took several deep breaths, then called downstairs. In a few moments, David appeared from the depths. "You're missing some good takeoffs," he said.

"Will you do me a favour?"

"Yes."

"My car's in for repair and I have to go out unexpectedly. Would you do me a great kindness and drive me across town? I'm not sure exactly where to go. Do you know where Parthenais is?"

They had to unearth David's street-guide in the glove compartment, then consult its small print as they drove along Sherbrooke in the persistent rain; the windows kept fogging over; it was difficult to see. Parthenais was well out toward the east end, past De Lorimier almost at D'Iberville. They turned south when they came to it, down the steep hill toward De

Maisonneuve. In a few minutes a massive dark shape stood up indistinctly before them, an ultra-modern office building four-teen stories high, in glassy black plastic siding, standing on a small plot of land surrounded by chain-link fence topped with multiple strands of shining barbed wire. It reminded him of a shiny polished dark monolith seen in some science-fiction film. Some sort of object of perverse worship. Close up, the building looked like most others built around 1969. They parked across the narrow street and approached the main entrance which opened into a spacious glassed-in hall two stories high, with an elevator bank to the right and a reception desk nearby. One or two guards idled in corners, paying no attention to them. He asked at the desk if he would be able to see Philly White, and the receptionist—perfectly agreeable and forthcoming—laughed jovially.

"Tomorrow, 1.30. Come back then."

"He seemed in pain or frightened. Could he be afraid of something?"

"Tomorrow, 1.30. Come back then."

One of the guards moved indecisively.

Time to get out of here while we still can, he thought. He felt great waves of imaginary fugitive guilt washing over him. Hundreds of movies lodged in his memory now rose up to frighten, to accuse. He thought of the fearful ending of *I Am a Fugitive from a Chain Gang* and hastened away. "What do you do, how do you live?" "I steal."

Driving homeward, David said, "I didn't care much for the atmosphere..."

He had to force himself to return the next afternoon. Just before he left the house, he got a call from a police sergeant in Dorval. "... heard from Philly White this morning—he's not a bad fellow, Philly, he wouldn't hurt anybody. He has no violence on his record."

"Record? What record?"

"Oh a long, long record. Four convictions in BC. Fraudulent

auto sales with forgery. Fraudulent roofing contracts. But no violence, I was glad when he told me he found a friend to help him out. If I come by your house, can I give you his radio? He left it in the cells here and I know he'll miss it. That Parthenais . . . it isn't like the Dorval Jail. It's no picnic, you bet." He recited a series of calamitous occurrences which had taken place at the detention centre. Group sucides, self-mutilations. "So you see if old Philly has a friend to help, I'll be glad. His family won't do nothing."

"His family aren't here. His mother is dead and they all live in Toronto."

"Did he tell you that? His mother lives in Montréal with one of his sisters and one brother. They don't go to see him. His wife and kids are here too."

"Does his wife know he's awaiting sentence?"

"No, she doesn't know a thing. . . nobody knows anything about Philly White for sure. Can I drop off his radio?"

"I'm not sure I'm going to be here. I have to go to the country. I have to go pick up my car. I don't believe I can make it; the family's expecting me back. I have to go and. . ."

"He'll be disappointed. He said you were coming down."

"He seems to say whatever he likes."

"That's right."

"Mail him the radio. I'll be away."

"No. No. I think I'll deliver it by hand."

The car was ready when he went over to get it. "It's ready; it's ready. You said it would be," he said happily; the garage-man looked at him in surprise.

"It always is."

"A pleasure. . . a pleasure."

The building on Parthenais looked more horrible in bright sunshine than in rainy darkness. Huge, slab-sided, far too glassy. Your gaze went right through it and out the other side. He went in, explained his errand to the man on the desk— the same man as the night before; didn't he ever sleep? And ascended to the tenth floor in an ordinary elevator. At the third, fifth and eighth floors it stopped automatically; he peered out without ostentation. Each floor seemed perfectly normal; you could see across the hall and out the windows. Ordinary office space. The view grew progressively more distant and spread-out as the car rose in the shaft. He was prepared for a hand-some prospect as he stepped out on ten, and was chilled and repelled by the barred, electrically-locked gate, the approaches beyond it to heavy steel doors. The four top floors of the build-ing form a maximum security jail. There is no exercise yard. There is no sports program. Prisoners may use one of three small recreation areas for periods of up to one hour, every second day, if they aren't receiving special discipline.

". . . you are not permitted to see him. What gave you the idea you could see him? Are you a relative?"

"No, he told me on the phone that. . ."

"I'm sorry, sir. His case is awaiting disposition. Only rela-tives."

"He told me he had no relatives nearer than Toronto."

"He told you a lie."

"Does his wife come to see him? How long has he been in here? I want to try to help."

"You aren't an officer of the John Howard Society?"

"No, nothing like that."

"Not a lawyer conferring with a judge about the sentence?"

"No, no."

The walls of this dreadful bullpen—a long counter or booth like that in a government liquor store or customs house—were painted a very pale grey-blue which did nothing to con-ceal their metallic chill. He began to look around wildly.

"What is your name, sir? Why did you come here?"

"This man called me on the telephone last night and told me he was in trouble; he didn't say how serious it was, but I gathered that he felt pretty desperate. . ."

". . . they'll all tell you that."

15

"Yes, I'm sure they will. I would myself, I think, if I had to stay here. Can't you tell me anything at all?"

"I've never seen the man."

"How do you know so much about him?"

"I'm simply following general regulations, sir."

"And he has no right to a visitor, like he claimed?"

"Certain relatives, his lawyer of record, officially authorized prison visitors."

"All right, then, a sergeant from Dorval is bringing in his radio. He left it there. Would you see that he gets it?"

"I don't know anything about that at all."

He left the bullpen and walked quickly through the massive doors. He felt very glad that they opened for him, that the elevator came, some time after he pressed the DOWN button. All the way out to the street and into the driver's seat of his car, he felt as if a hand might descend on his shoulder. There was a parking ticket under the left windshield wiper. The rubberized gorilla mask smiled up at him from where he had dropped it on the front seat. He felt intensely happy to see it there, happy that he'd remembered it, that his children enjoyed having it. He made the best of his way out of town.

The mask alone was not enough, naturally. Four imaginative new costumes were required. The boys decided to go out as soldiers of the American Civil War, one in blue uniform, one in grey; design and fitting of these intricate costumes occupied much of September and early October.

"What are you going out as?"

"Soldiers of the War Between the States, as they would have been dressed at Gettysburg." The younger son was a student of Civil War history and a bitter partisan of the North, an admirer of Lincoln and Grant.

"But don't you think Lee was the greatest general of that war?"

"He lost, didn't he?"

Not much to be said to that.

16

And of course, he reflected, on the essential issue of slavery the North had been in the right. He was certain of that; what could possibly be urged in favour of slavery, of imprisonment, detention, referral to clinic? He felt mixed up, his head crowded with civilized misgiving. He started to get letters addressed to Philly White, in his care. He wouldn't open them and couldn't decide what to do with them. Some were post-marked Vancouver. One looked like an Income Tax refund cheque. A month after the first phone call, there came another.

"Yes, it's me. I want to thank you for everything you've done for me. Sergeant Bastien told me how you helped him."

"The man from Dorval with your radio."

"He said how kind you were."

"Were you actually talking to Sergeant Bastien?" It had become important to extract some unambiguous, verifiable statement.

"Not actually talking to him in so many words. . . exactly."

"How then?"

"Well, he got through to me all right. These veteran police officers have ways of dealing with things that you and I wouldn't think of."

"I didn't do anything for you, White. I have no intention of doing anything for you." He at least could be unambiguous, or hoped he could.

"But you came down to the Prevention Centre to see me, didn't you?"

"I did. Anybody would have done that."

"But you came twice, didn't you?"

"How do you know?"

"I know." There was a noxious appeal to this way of talking. He felt himself being drawn into the position of co-conspirator and even accomplice. He had enough free-floating fear of having done something criminal in his imagination without this.

"Just handle my mail for me," begged White.

17

"Why can't it go directly to jail?" He felt dreadfully like laughing. He thought, "Go directly to Jail; do not pass GO; do not collect $200"; he remembered the cards in the pile marked "Get out of Jail free."

"Would you like your wife to have to send her letters to such a place?"

"No."

"Do this for me then, for the sake of the old days."

"What old days? Do you know, I can barely remember you. That's 40 years ago. I don't have any responsibility for you."

"We are all responsible for one another," said White.

"Then why did you... never mind."

"I can use your address?"

"I'll forward anything that arrives."

The call was abruptly ended by that strange echoing click suggestive of constant switchboard surveillance. He wondered who was listening, and thought of making misleading and ambiguous remarks the next time White telephoned, just to give the listeners something to think about, realizing at the same moment that such an action would cause them to set up a dossier on him, which would then have the assured and interminable existence of an official file.

A flood of correspondence ensued, much of it from distant provinces, all addressed to his quiet Montréal street, all for Philly White. He would wait for three or four days till he had a dozen or so items, then bundle them together in a single large envelope and forward it to Parthenais Street. Certain letters obviously got through to White, who discussed them in later phone calls. Some were perhaps suppressed by the authorities or censored by them, but on the whole White seemed well abreast of his outside affairs; he had now been at the Centre de Prevention for August, September, most of October—almost thirteen weeks; this was nothing compared to the detention of other unfortunates. The top floors were designed to hold 250 inmates, all in one way or another of special status.

Either they could not be brought to trial because the prosecutor's case was incomplete, or the dockets were overburdened, or their lawyers were evading the event for tactical reasons: those in this last category might wait forever without their process coming on. Many died on Parthenais Street without receiving either condemnation or justification. And there were always more than 300 crowded into the cells.

There were many like White whose guilt had been legally established. Convicted, criminals in the eyes of the law, sentenced, as yet undisposed of, they could not be conveniently put away and forgotten in this or that prison because a humane penology wished to "cure" them—in White's case apparently to dry the liquor out of him and begin treatment for alcoholism. A cured alcoholic, he might no longer be a fraud-artist and con-man, but this was doubtful. The alcoholism and the pathological addiction to lying might be elements of deeper ruin, probably were.

Nobody knows what is truly criminal, who are culpable. There are legal definitions, always abstract, inexact. There is observably bad—at least socially unacceptable—behaviour: what is called the "psychopathic personality" where social responsibility is rejected together with the possibility of truthfulness. What oppressed the listener to Philly White's phone calls was that he never, even by accident, said the plain truth.

Disguise abounded; cold came on. Toward the end of the month the boys completed their Civil War costumes and began to parade around the house in them, looking from a short distance wonderfully authentic. The younger lad had constructed one of those flat, forward-slanting Confederate caps with a badge of crossed rifles over the peak, and the letters C.S.A. sewn into it irregularly. The effect was truly persuasive. He had a cardboard musket and a water bottle. He kept saying, "Pickett's charge represented the high-water mark of the Confederacy," and his father never managed to establish what that meant. The other boy had decided to approach the northern

19

infantryman's dress with less historical correctness and more freedom of interpretation. He carried a powder-horn—more appropriate for the Revolutionary War—and wore a shaggy false beard made of stuff chopped from an old Borghana coat of their mother's, which gave him an unexpectedly Russian air.

The girls hovered over alternatives. Then in a late fury of artistic creation they evolved two superb and original designs. For the younger girl, the baby of the family, they made a horse's body from a painted and draped cardboard carton fitted around her waist like an Eskimo's kayak. This was completed by floppy artificial legs hanging from a painted saddle—a caricature of a circus equestrienne. Her sister had then simply to dress herself as a ringmaster: red coat, tall hat, white breeches, riding whip, and the illusion was perfect and striking.

Mixed images of strangely-caparisoned, smallish persons capering around him wound their way into their father's worried judgment. All day on the 31st of the month he lazed around the house among orange and black festoons, expecting some sort of resolution of the affair of White the bunco steerer. The weekend before, all clocks had been put back. It was full dark by six pm. The children departed for their exciting annual night walk, gangs of neighbourhood kids beginning to press the doorbell. The phone rang in the midst of other urgent pealings, as he raised his coffee cup to his lips. Of course it was his old friend on Parthenais Street, with his first concrete demand for money. "If you'll just make the one payment for me, $184.80, we can retain ownership, they won't repossess. It's in the wife's name. I'll tell you where to send your cheque, and thanks for what you're trying to do. I really mean it."

He felt great anger squeezing his throat. "You don't mean it at all," he said, "you're just trying it on. I knew it would get to this point. A hundred and eighty from the poor sucker for openers, eh? It's finished, White, you get me? That's it. Don't call again and don't have any more mail sent here. I thought

you needed me. I thought you meant it. All just a big con.
You're still at it even though they've locked you up. You've
been sentenced. How come they don't put you where you belong?"

"*They're* trying to help me."

"Let them! Whoever *they* are."

"I'm only trying to make contact."

"Good-bye White. Don't call again."

He hoped the listeners got it all; there wouldn't be any more
calls. The doorbell rang and he walked through the house,
opened the door and confronted a small visitant dressed as a
ghost. He handed this person many sugary treats, then shut the
door. I did right, he told himself, I did right (wrong), I did
right, right (wrong), I did right. . .

Socks and Boots

"... a natural pair," Noreen Mallory

I: SOCKS

Domenico Lercaro got here by himself—from Calabria—and it wasn't easy. The effort left him bewildered and almost broke, unable to speak the same dialect as the rest of the Italians in town, and terribly cold in winter. Where he came from there were no jobs. All the young men from his birthplace on the Gulf of Taranto had moved north, some of them very far north, but none had come as far as he had.

He had not counted on our climate.

At the same time he could not wish himself back home. It had been too much of nothing, an unchanging metallic sky, crazily turbulent weather, an everlasting feeling of being at the extreme edge of the world, neither in winter nor summer, a place where it was always March, where the wind never stopped, seeming to blow the people away from around you. His village was a widening in a wobbly hillside track inhabited by 23 men and women, an indeterminate number of children, and eight goats. He walked away and walked away north. . . north. . . took him two years to get where his work was paid for in money. Always before he had been paid in mere existence.

In Torino there were posters about Canada showing tulips, grass, lakes, boats, cities lit up at night and girls in bathing suits. He formed a mental picture of this country which was uncritical because he had nothing to compare it with except what he had left. Canada was "America" and there were millions of Italians over there. Twice he saw movies of America at a worker's club in the automotive assembly plant where he worked, and what impressed him was the speed with which everybody talked and the way in which all the space in the pictures was filled with straight lines. This made him aware of the disorganization in his own history, the blankness of what had happened to him so far, which frightened him more each time he thought of it.

Domenico Lercaro was not stupid, not unhealthy, not naturally inarticulate though he almost never spoke. He was not brutal, mean, inhumane. It was hard to say what he was. A range of possibilities, an unopened box, raw consciousness, what? He was a spot in civilization where nothing happened to be going on, just like his village, somewhere unconsidered, not worth seizing and taking trouble over, unexploitable because off to one side of ordinary wealth.

He hummed much of the time, making an unusual music without rhythm or clear intervals or words to accompany it. If anybody had listened to this loud humming, which you couldn't hear in the assembly plant, it would have sounded like unmixed life. He enjoyed the vibration of his vocal cords and the resonance in his nose and mouth and the way he could modify the sounds he made. He kept his mouth closed. Over three or four years he composed about a dozen hums—some of them surprisingly long. After he had made up enough of them to respond to most of what happened to him, he stopped inventing new ones.

He would go for peculiar walks, first hup-hup-hupping up and down on his heels like a walker in Olympic competition, then swinging his legs smooth and straight like a runner in slow motion, then trying to see how long he could walk without taking breath. Humming and walking became the book of his experience. You could hum in many ways (how many —twelve, fifteen?) and you could walk in five ways. This knowledge gave him a basis for various comparisons, and on simple comparisons more complicated ones could be built. He now saw that he did not have to work in the assembly plant because he had some money. Some. There was America and straight lines.

We were admitting Italians to Canada in large numbers so he came here. The streets were rectilinear once you got away from the dockside, which was irregular and distressful to him. Off the ship and through immigration, he walked uptown as fast as he could, using the most important of the five ways to walk, the way that gets you somewhere fast. He had not been able to walk far enough on the ship to feel in full control of himself. His first day in Montréal he walked seventeen miles and after a while began to see signs in Italian. He knew some Piedmontese now and even some Tuscan and could figure out the signs—they were in more or less standard Italian and he could read very well when he wanted to. He got a room in northeastern Montréal and made comparisons: this is a big room, three times as big as my room in Torino; there are some Fiats on the roads but more Volkswagens and many more American cars; not all Italians live on pasta. I never did. This is America; Montréal, Canada, America, it is very warm.

He began to see that an organized life might be a falsified life—construction work or gardening seemed to be the work options open. This seemed very limiting as he had never done either. He had hated heights since infancy, associating vertigo with his native village and the pressure of wind in his ears. Growing things in the soil was something he knew nothing about. He had never known anybody who did such a thing. He had swept floors and pushed heavy metal carts with cylinder blocks in them. What he could do was stay on his feet for a long time and push something. His tools were his feet, which he cared for meticulously, his socks and his boots.

So he walked, walked looking, having trouble explaining himself to foremen in metropolitan Italian. He knew no French. Got a job as a helper on a grocery truck, lasted ten weeks. He dropped boxes and broke eggs. He learned to smile often. Got a job as a garbageman; this was closer. For this you

24

had to run and lift, which was like walking and pushing, so he could hold it. Was a garbageman for a long time. Winter came: sheer horror. The metal handles of the garbage cans froze to his hands and pulled the skin off. The crew was paid so much per street, according to their contract with the city, so they ran and ran and did the allotted streets in three-quarters the contracted time, so they'd have free time not to run. On the garbage crew Domenico always suspected that it would be better to walk for eight hours than run for six, but he was incapable of expressing the idea or defending it. He ran the whole winter with frozen hands and knew that there was something better he could do. This was his first reflective, considered choice, and it changed him. He had no previous conception of a winter so long and so cold.

In the spring he married a Piedmontese girl named Vanna DiConto who immediately gave his life a structure so multiform that he felt yanked all at once out of insignificance into determined manhood. She taught him some English, a little French, put his socks away to mend them and lined up his workboots in a row—four boots. She bought him some nylon socks which never got holes in them; they felt cold and slippery on his feet, and when he wore them on the job all day they burned his skin. There was no give to them. Talk about socks became a constant element in his relations with his wife. She did not seem to understand how important his feet were. She wanted to discuss her own feet, which were always cold in bed. This was a surprise because the rest of her was always intensely warm. When he got into bed beside her she radiated heat which he found so pleasing that he would sometimes say something about it.

"But my feet are cold," Vanna would answer, grumbling like a child.

That summer the garbage stank, fermenting and liquefying in cans and cartons: scrapings of plates, clotted grease and hair, disposable diapers. Domenico shone with sweat. How could it be so cold, then so warm? In July he was afflicted by a hateful minor ailment, a rankly acid sweat that burned and itched between his toes, thickening and glistening on the flat surfaces of the big toe and the second, on either foot, searing the skin and blistering it an unhealthy white and red. He could hardly stand, much less walk, and was afraid of the smell from his feet and the greasy oily feel of the strange sweat.

Vana advised bathing four times a day, constant changes of socks, then boracic acid powder. In the end the infection went away, but its effects left distrust between man and wife.

"How they stink," Vanna said, holding a pair of his socks at arm's length. She grimaced. He thought she was very pretty and felt attacked. He quit the garbage crew and spent two terrifying months looking for another job, something clean, nothing involving dirt and sweat, in the cold. He got a new job in November, good for four months. Labourer on a snow-removal gang.

These gangs are like armoured divisions, with many motorized vehicles operating according to a rigorous system. First comes the little truck that puts out the NO PARKING signs, then the tiny one-man tractor that scrapes the sidewalk, then the heavy equipment, the large plow that piles the snow and ice in enormous hillocks on one side of the road, the gigantic rotary sweeper with its blower shaft hanging up over a dump-truck which rides slowly along under the blower till it is full —then it moves ahead, away down the street, to be replaced by an empty truck. Behind the heavy equipment another small tractor turns and darts, trimming the curbs and sidewalks. The heaviest fall of snow can be disposed of like this in around 48 hours, even including obscure side streets.

When Domenico joined the gang he saw these mighty engines lined up in a yard, as if marshalled for parade, drivers at the ready, labourers and foremen in attendance. He felt awe. But that first awe was nothing to what he felt during blizzards. Weather predictions were closely monitored by city authori-

26

ties: first flakes, tentative and idle in early afternoon, could be recognized immediately as the gestures of an infant snow-storm. Orders went out. Sanding trucks and light sweeping and salting gangs started work. As night fell and the snow came thicker, first plowing began, then more determined plowing. For 24 hours the gangs fought a holding operation. Then the snow would stop—eight inches, ten inches, twelve, not often more—the sun would appear. Cold might grow intense. Now came the great crews, the concentrated effort to clear off the streets before more snow came. We can live with twelve inches: 24 is something else. At that point traffic patterns break down, commerce is disrupted, criminality doubles. Round the clock shifts, overtime, action.

Frozen feet.

Domenico was inexperienced and lucky to have the job at all. They made him lantern man. His work consisted of backing up slowly in front of the great rotary sweeper, not too far in front of it, especially at night, along the top of the snow hills with a red lantern, to give the operator of the sweeper a line to follow in the middle of the storm of flying ice chips and sprayed slush.

Two years before in Winnipeg a child playing on such a snow hill had been gobbled up by a sweeper and cut to pieces by the powerful blades inside the mechanism which ground the iced snow into powder. Domenico didn't know this. What he knew was that he was now the servant of an immensely strong and active machine whose piercing cry was the sound of a divine beast. As he backed unevenly along the snow hills he sometimes felt a crazy wish to throw himself into the mouth of the sucking sweeper which snouted toward him. When his feet sank too deeply into heavy wet snow he was in extreme danger of which he was completely unaware. He heard the roar and grind and crunch and surrendered himself to some-thing unspeakable.

Twelve hours of this taxed his strength viciously. He went

home and took off his boots and emptied them. They were caked with dirty ice which took a while to melt. His socks were soaking, matted into hurtful lumps of coarse knitted yarn, sometimes wool, more often some artificial fabric. When the roaring and crashing of the rotary sweeper had died out of his ears, he would get up from his chair, find a towel and chafe his ankles and feet, which hurt badly. He would think of thick dry warm woollen socks without holes. It made him frantic to think how long it was that Vanna took to darn his socks. She never darned his socks. She said they stank. He wanted them dry and new.

He saw that darning his socks was servitude for her. His dirt and wet and smell repelled her. Two o'clock in the morning. He dried himself and prepared for bed, went into the bedroom and lit a shaded lamp. Vanna was sound asleep under heavy blankets. Domenico went to the window and peered out; a new fall was beginning, early flakes swirling, more overtime on the way. He turned to the bed and twitched back the blankets, then straightened up amazed. His wife's feet protruded from under the bedclothes, and on them were thick warm dry woollen socks without holes. His.

He shook all over his body and raised his arms above his head, his mouth opened in a strained circle, a silent howl. He took a quick involuntary step toward the sleeping woman. His heart burned with resentment.

II: BOOTS

My wife pays no attention to fashion, which is something to be thankful for, so when she complained again and again about her cold wet feet I knew she wasn't joking.

"Nobody makes good snowboots for women," she kept saying.

"They must."

"No they don't. I've looked and looked this past two winters and I can't find anything. It's a conspiracy."

I said, "Conspiracy theories are the paranoia of intellectuals."

"I'm no intellectual," she said truthfully.

I never knew her to take this line before, attributing the cause of a personal problem to some invisible group of evil planners. She brooded about it. She said, "It's the international conspiracy of the snowboot manufacturers, possibly a cartel with connections on both sides of the iron curtain."

"Tell me all about it."

"About twenty years ago," she began, "a girl used to be able to buy galoshes. You remember, they were usually black, made of some kind of waterproof fabric with a rubber sole and heel, and those funny little clip fasteners. You could get them low-cut or you could get them so they came halfway up your calf. They had a beige lining, felt or velour. I had one pair after another when I was growing up, and now I have this problem about my feet I can see that my infantile galoshes formed a primordial image for me. Warm, fuzzy, soft. My mother would snap them on, give me a kiss, and send me out to play in the snow. You don't know what it was like around our house in the old days. I was the only girl my age in the neighbourhood, and the only playmate I had was two years older, Paddy Ann Devlin. She used to pinch me. She used to refuse to play with me."

I could see that these reminiscences were about to pass into a familiar track. "You've told me all about Paddy Ann," I said. "I've even met her. I don't see what she has to do with snowboots."

"I associate warm snowboots with Paddy Ann," my wife said. "She often had coloured ones but mine were always black."

"Never mind that."

"I won't. I'll put that aside."

"You're very wise."

"Do you know, I've been all over town looking for something I could wear over my shoes. All they make these days are little slip-on things that won't go over a shoe, no matter what size you buy; they just aren't designed to. You're supposed to carry a pair of shoes or slippers with you—an awful nuisance—and when you get where you're going, you take your boots off, get out your shoes, put them on, leave the boots to dry. When you're leaving you take your shoes off—and your feet always get dirty standing on the mat or the floor—the bottoms of your stockings get black—put the boots on, put the shoes in the bag. . . not only that, they won't keep your feet dry, the way they're cut. I haven't had a pair of winter boots in years that would keep water out. I don't say they leak, but the tops are cut wrong. They sacrifice comfort to looks."

"Who do?"

"The snowboot cartel."

"There is no snowboot cartel," I said. "Why can't you simply buy a pair of whatever's available, only a size larger so you can wear shoes under?"

"Impossible. The way the last is shaped a shoe won't go inside unless you get them three sizes too big, and then you get snow down inside because they flop around."

"Really?"

"Certainly really! Do you think I'm making this up?"

"No. I don't think that. I tell you what I do think though. If there's a demand for an article, somebody must be supplying it. What you appear to want is a simple, well-cut boot, with a last wide enough to take your shoes inside, and an upper designed so that snow won't come in over top. Right?"

"Exactly."

"Somebody must be selling them."

"Uh-uh."

"Come on now, somebody must. You've just missed them; you can't have looked. In this affluent society. . ."

She looked dangerous, so I stopped.

"There is no such boot," she said.

"Must be."

"No."

"I never heard of such a thing," I said. "Here, get me the Eaton's fall sale catalogue. No, not the toy catalogue. No, not the big catalogue. That's it, the sale catalogue. Let's see."

I thumbed through the book for a while, then finally consulted the index.

"Here we are. 'Women's winter footwear.' Now we'll see."

I picked out something in a brown suede effect that looked very attractive. Women's boots mean nothing to me ordinarily.

"They look very nice. How much do we want to spend?"

"Not over $12. You can't get a shoe in those."

I looked at the description of the article and she was right. Not only that, there wasn't a pair of boots on the page that would take a shoe. "That's extremely interesting," I said. It opened up a world of speculation. "I wonder why that is."

"I can't tell you that," she said, "but it's discriminatory. All I want is a comfortable snowboot, and I can't get it."

"Why don't you buy a pair of men's workboots, shearling-lined, like those ones I bought in Hartford? They're ten years old and as good as new. I'll never wear them out. Every winter you go over the soles and welts with one of those silicone waterproofings. Keep you dry as a bone."

But she has the idea that her feet are on the big side. I don't think they are. I think they're cute little feet but I can't convince her. Her attitude to her feet is more projective than descriptive.

"Don't be a fool," she said curtly.

"I'm quite serious. If you don't want to wear workboots for cosmetic reasons. . ."

"It isn't that."

"You're a sensible woman. If the heavy workboots with the shearling-pile lining, warm felt insole, water-resistant Neo-prene sole and heel, don't meet your specifications. . ."

"Stop that," she said, her mouth watering.

". . . look around and pick out another kind of man's boot. What does it matter how they look? You're wearing them for comfort and warmth, not to impress anybody. Who looks at your overshoes anyway?"

"Could we go as high as $15?"

"Why not? Go around to some of the smaller stores; maybe they've got something in stock from years back." I thought that would be the end of it.

Well sir, she did it, something hardly anybody does any-more. Patronized the neighbourhood merchants, went the length of the shopping district along Sherbrooke from Girou-ard to Hampton. Our neighbourhood. Also the stores around Cavendish and Somerled: picture framers, music stores, pet shops, paint and wallpaper, those specialized little places that you look in sometimes as you pass, wondering how they stay in business. The neighbourhood. We should be more loyal to our neighbourhoods. I'm going to start buying my clothes in the district if I can find what I want.

My wife couldn't find what she wanted. She had a whole sequence of upsetting meetings with local merchants. They wouldn't, literally *wouldn't*, sell her what she wanted.

"I was in the Fit-Rite Shoestore, corner Kensington, this afternoon," she told me.

"Any good boots?"

"Do you know what that man said? He said, 'Madam, your problem is simply you've been buying a cheaper article. I've got just the thing for you.' Then he went in the back of the store and was gone fifteen minutes. I figured he was digging out some item he'd had in inventory for years, that he was going to try to stick me with. Maybe I would unearth some rare pair of overshoes, like an archaeologist on a dig."

"What happened?"

"He came back with a pair of sealskin boots. Everybody knows about sealskin boots for Heaven's sake. I could get them anywhere. I'm perfectly familiar with them."

"Look how smart," he said. "Neat. Small-looking, thong ties. You could wear them anywhere, don't need a shoe underneath. Soft and clinging."

"How much?"

"To you, $39.95."

"It was the 'to you' that annoyed me," she said. "I gave it to him good. I said, 'What am I, rich or something? Do I look rich to you? I want a pair of galoshes, man, not a pair of hand-tailored gloves for my feet. What kind of a lunatic pays $40 for that? Do you mean to stand there and tell me you can't meet the demand?' I was a bit rude, I think."

"I'm sorry, Madam," he said. "We get no call for the kind of thing you're talking about. Mind you, mind you, I'm not saying we shouldn't; we used to sell a flock of them. Not for ten years. I blame the Beatles."

"What does your own wife wear?"

"She takes from stock. $40 boots."

My wife said, "I felt sorry for the man, and went out of the store thinking, 'Do unto others as you would have them do unto you.'"

I said, "That's a great line but you can't make it stick. It seems wrong, somehow, that you have to pay $40 to get something good-looking and comfortable. I mean, lots of people can't pay $40. We can't. At least, I mean, go ahead if you want to, but it's uneconomical."

"That's just it. It isn't right that nobody's making them.

33

Not *right*. Somebody ought to."

I said, "I don't think fashion has anything to do with morals."

"Oh, but you're so wrong. Fashion makes morals."

"I thought it was the other way around."

"No, no, no, a human being who is fool enough to wear a girdle and bra can only behave in certain ways—submissive, dependent, silly, and it's the same with snowboots. Soft and clinging! I don't know why we put up with it. I don't know why I wear these canvas and net bags on my tits. For one thing, they never fit right."

"It's none of my business but you can leave them off anytime as far as I'm concerned."

"Maybe I will," she said, looking fierce.

I expected her to strike a blow for the new feminism at almost any time, probably in the form of refusal to wear an irrationally-designed and otiose garment, nylon stockings or absurdly narrow shoes. But instead she continued to campaign on the snowboot issue, going into stores and making scenes when they refused to allow her to buy men's galoshes. "You haven't any idea. . . the prejudice, the taboos," she told me, "these men actually refuse to sell me something I want to buy. Refuse!"

"Should I go with you sometime? Between the two of us we could overpower the clerk and escape with the goods."

"Don't tease, sweetie, there's a principle involved."

When a clever woman uses the word "principle" there's trouble in store for somebody. I hoped it wasn't me. Instead it was the owner of the Fit-Rite Shoestore, a special object of her anger. One early winter afternoon she walked into his place and ordered him to sell her the men's overshoes in the window. Calf-length, brown rubber, cut narrow with a good thick ring of synthetic fur around the inside of the uppers, and big enough to get a shoe inside.

The poor man cringed and pleaded. "I can't let you wear

those out of the store, Madam, I just can't. I refuse to. Don't do it, please!" He tried to restrain her but she overcame him, seized the footwear, flung $7.95 plus tax on a showcase and departed.

Those boots are on their third winter now, and she's never had a pair she liked better. Goes around with a happy smile and dry feet. Now, two years later, we're beginning to see similar boots on many other women, perhaps a sign of a new, moral, fashion. I ask myself, will women abandon unreasonable adornment? The idea upsets me.

A Near Miss

Supposed to be an aide of the counter-revolutionary hero for whom this town was named, a young lieutenant with varnished beige cheeks shines in the dark, an ancestral portrait from Mother's side of the family. Tight embroidered collar, red coat, pop eyes, varnish. Last week I caught Mother cleaning him with lemon oil.

"It's my heirloom after all. He was Lieutenant Dunglas, a cousin of my great great grandmother, very close to General Brock."

"Who can have painted it?"

"It's my heirloom, Marnie."

"It won't be for long if you clean it with lemon oil."

"Miss Smartie."

The lemon oil was meant for the dining-room table, gleam and sheen of oak veneer, not an heirloom, an $80 table with extra leaves, seating twelve at its fullest extent. My plate is eternally set down over a crack between leaves, wobbling as I stare at it, even with a thick pad under the fine linen table-cloth. I hate a wobbling plate.

"Give the child more, David. She's always such a picky eater."

"I AM NOT PICKY." Now my plate wobbles under a load of pan-roasted potatoes and steaming beef. "I can't eat all that."

Dad would say: "Eat what you can, and give God thanks."

Why was the piano in the dining-room? It certainly took up a lot of room and was never moved; whoever sat at that end of the table, beside the carver, bumped his elbow continually

36

unless he was left-handed. "Southpaws are goofy." That would be Cousin Dal from Perth Amboy, Dal McCredie, pronounced McCruddy. We had long chains of dangling relatives from the States because the family moved here after the Revolution— hence the pop-eyed counter-revolutionary lieutenant. He spoiled my Sunday dinner for years because I brooded about his origins. He wore an inaccurately rendered medal, one of the earliest such awards of the British Army, the size of a silver dollar with a watered-silk ribbon in striped purple, black and crimson. "Lefties have a screw loose, take Lefty Gomez." That makes me think of boxtops; when he visited us in the summer Dal McCruddy always wanted boxtops. He would leer at me: "How's your Puffed Rice, kiddo?" He was the last boy I knew who said "kiddo." I hated him; he was a rube.

"The lefty sits in the corner."

"All right Dal, we'll manage." We'd jump when Uncle Phil McCredie struck a treble chord cutting his meat. "I see what you mean."

Lemon oil made the table shine deep and dark in the leafy sunshine flooding through the verandah door and the window over the buffet. When did the piano get into the dining-room? ". . . and give God thanks."

One afternoon about five o'clock, when I was fifteen, my father caught me shaving my legs in the bathroom, bent over with one knee jabbed into my stomach, breathless. I had not tried this before; it was his razor naturally and I hadn't got a very firm lather. The floor of the bathroom was soaking, and my feet kept slipping on the edge of the tub.

"You want a thicker lather on that," he said suddenly, making me jump. My foot shot off the edge of the tub and I might have fallen awkwardly, but he caught me and lifted me, setting my feet on the bathmat. "Adventures in the bathroom," he said, "you can get killed in here, lots do. They're in the office all the time with nicks and lumps and abrasions, and electrocutions which I can't do much about."

"I'll get you some fresh blades for your birthday, Daddy. I think I've spoiled this one. It doesn't cut anything."

"Marnie, there's nothing to cut."

Sometime before I had seen Zsa Zsa Gabor in a TV commercial, flourishing this instrument and explaining how chic she felt with hairless legs. I see now that the whole conception was vile, but I was a very silly girl at fifteen. Repugnance to visible body hair possessed me for a week, and I went over myself from one end to the other scraping and smoothing. The memory makes me laugh. I was never really very hairy. My hair is too light and fine to be easily seen, I'm told, but at that time I was smoother in the armpits than any girl in my class; we compared in the lockers.

"Why are you doing that?"

"Personal daintiness," I said rebelliously, and he leaned against the door and laughed and laughed. At first I was mad and then it began to seem funny to me too. "It is silly, isn't it?"

"You'll never be any daintier than nature intended, Marnie, which in your case is dainty enough. Have you been watching television?"

"Ummmm-hmmmm."

"Zsa Zsa isn't it, or one of those?"

"She."

"Ah well, that explains it. I believe there's more tulle in that commercial than I've seen in some time."

"Chiffon."

"Tulle, chiffon. She's got something to hide behind those clouds. Never worry about what you see in TV commercials, Marnie, life's too short, and we can assume them to be false."

"Them all?"

"Ah, now and then they deviate into sense."

The lather grew powdery on my legs. "I'd better finish what I'm doing."

"A wise habit. But after this, leave your legs as they are;

38

they're dainty enough. Any daintier and you'd cruelly eclipse the rest of your sex."

"Shouldn't I be as dainty as possible?"

"I wonder what that word means, actually?" he said abstractedly. "No, as a matter of fact it's sometimes kindest to be a shade less clean and fresh than is theoretically possible, so the rest of us aren't shamed."

There was no question of his expecting me to take this in at fifteen; it's nevertheless true that I got most of my education from him.

"You expect too much." Did she say it as succinctly as I remember or is my memory editing the conversation? Mimsy was not especially succinct for a roommate, though as free with criticism as the general run. I had some ghastly roommates: Flora's morals, Rosemary and her boyfriend the forester, but Mimsy was just a nice Brockville girl like me. We had foundered in the same low-comedy dinghy during a regatta, had been in and out of each other's houses since babyhood, and I was lucky to have her for a roommate the last two years. People don't understand what a spiritless death-ridden hole Whitney Hall —or any women's residence—must be. I am *so* glad I'm out, and if I ever again have to pass a night in a room with stuffed animals, I'll vomit on them.

Flora had a panda she made love to, a great black and white thing from her cradle, you never saw anything like it, lover, companion, father, mother and friend. She used to go to sleep sucking her thumb and cuddling this thing. Rosemary had only smallish teddy bears, but then she had a box of sachet with a celluloid doll in an evening dress for a top; you felt like you were drowning in oopsies. But Mimsy was just a clean simple girl. "You expect too much."

"Ah, what do you mean, Mimsies?"

"Marnie, they're just boys, that's all they are."

"When do we get to the men? Are there no men around this university? The athletes want Mommy; the actors want

39

each other, God knows why. The campus politicians want to be loved without requital. Where are the men?"

"Oh you make me sick, the way you pick holes in everything. With your clothes and looks, you should be Top Girl."

"You're kidding. You are kid-ding. I am a lump, lump, lump."

"Going to lectures, taking copious notes. . . there's our buzzer. Be nice to them now, because even if you don't want them, perhaps I do."

"Both?"

"A choice."

"Where are they taking us?"

"Beer and dancing."

"I can't face it."

"You've got to. Smile and show your dimple. Come on, now, here we go. It's easy Marn. Be nice, ah, be nice."

She had picked one of them up—I think Harasymchuk—in the Baldwin Street Market—where she used to go for fresh carrots, her one original independent act. While arguing with peddlers and fending off amorous chicken-pluckers, she had met Harasymchuk and gone for coffee trailing clouds of carrots.

"Bring a friend. I got a nice roommate; she should be Top Girl."

"My friend does figure studies."

"No, that's out."

"What's out?"

"Posing."

He laughed at her. "She couldn't do it. It's terribly hard work and none of you bitches knows what hard work is."

Mimsy was full of this for days. "He called me a bitch, Marnie, to my face and, you know, I liked it."

"All right, all right, I'll go with you."

"Hooray."

So here we are walking two miles to a beerhall on a cheap

date, which is all right by me, I don't expect too much. Dad taught me that poor men are sometimes just as nice as people like us, but I was about eighteen before he began to get this into my head. In Brockville the only poor people I ever saw were ones who walked in to school from the incest-ridden back concessions, with holey clothes and dirty noses. I played with them at recess but we didn't walk home together.

"Being what I am, Marnie, I limit your views. You mustn't judge the world by the people on our block; plenty of people who look funny when you meet them are quite intelligent, quite responsible, when you get to know them, even very poor people, even sick old ones. I don't know that I've done right by you, bringing you up in this atmosphere."

"You give me everything I want."

"There must be something I can't give you?"

"What?"

"Think! Maybe you're a bit young."

"I'm nineteen."

"And what don't you have?"

"Do you mean a husband?"

"You can get a husband any time. Blessed are they who hunger and thirst after justice, for they shall be filled. When I was a young man, I was miserably poor; my practice paid me nothing for years. It was the Depression—you wouldn't remember. Men in my class, trained engineers, even some doctors, couldn't work at what they had been trained for, without going hungry. Nobody in this town had any money to pay me. Those who did didn't call me in, but went to the established men, no discredit to them, I've been poor, your mother has been poor."

"Being a doctor and poor is different from just being poor."

"You put your finger on the sore place. There's much injustice, much pain and hunger, in this world, and many poor. Do they teach you that nowadays at the university?"

"Nobody's said anything so far."

"And you've everything you want, short of a husband. Ah

41

well, sweetheart, we'll let it go, I don't mean to spoil a holiday weekend. Tell me about those painters, or better still, come and play the piano and we'll sing."

We went into the dining-room and fished out *Everybody's Favourite Songbook*. Lieutenant Dunglas glared familiarly over our shoulderblades and it grew dark behind us and I thought about what he'd said.

"I'll bet there isn't a painting in Brockville, not what you'd call a painting."

"And you'd be so wrong. We have a painting in our dining-room." I never got to like Harasymchuk though Mimsy loved him, really loved him I think, at least to hear her tell it.

"I just melt when he looks at me."

"Mimsy, for Heaven's sake. Men are all alike, the younger ones. They're all interested in the one thing."

"Stop kidding," she said, shivering. I stopped but kept a close eye on the painters.

"What kind of painting would you have in your dining-room?" He turned to Jack Reed, sitting beside us. "Marnie is the squarest girl in Toronto, a natural-born Progressive Conservative." He had that on me. I had belonged to the young Progressive-Conservatives for a while, betrayed into it by a moribund boyfriend, a black mark against me on the hipsters' blacklist; they're great for blacklists, they're as illiberal as anyone else. Of course Harasymchuk didn't like me. He was always proclaiming himself a Hunky off the streets of Parkdale, a self-made poor boy who had fought his way up through the art courses at Central Tech.

"Coward," I said. I can spot attracted aggression quick enough.

He said: "She thinks her shit doesn't stink," squinting at me and I felt disgusted, and oddly excited; nobody I knew talked like that, or at least he was the first. Three nights later, blind with four hours' beer-drinking, we came out of the Lundy's

42

Lane at closing time, walked away from the others and stood in a dark doorway where we clutched each other blindly and kissed in a furious mixture of dislike and passion. Nothing ever came of it, and I never boasted to Mimsy that I could have had Ted Harasymchuk for a watchcharm any time I wanted. All our last two years in residence that mean snarky little rat gave poor Mimsy a bad time, just because he was afraid I'd turn him in.

Then the last May we were in school he said: "Go ahead and tell her; we're all through anyway."

"Tell who what?"

"Tell your little roommate I gave you a bit of the old slap and tickle in a doorway one time, not even a one-night stand."

"Settle your sordid little messes your own way," I said, "and get out of my way."

"You never told me about the painting in your dining-room." He grabbed me by the wrist. I think he was sorry to see things end.

"A primitive," I said, "you wouldn't understand it, but it's beter than your stuff." That was a lie because he's good, damn him, as good as there is around, so Paul says.

"What kind of a primitive?"

"An ancestral portrait of an army officer, a decent man, not like you. You can tell from the picture."

"You're going to explain a picture to me, are you?"

"I know a real man when I see one."

"And they're all in the pictures on the wall, aren't they?" That made me think.

I know I'm not a pretty woman, which is hard to say because it sounds like dreadful false modesty, but it's true. It's very hard for a girl to assess herself that way; you go on hoping everything will come out right. Your ankles will slim out with exercise and diet, but without knobs. You'll hit just the colours that make you look your best, and when you're older you'll learn how to wear clothes. The hope is always there that since every woman has the attraction of her sex—sitting on a gold-mine as the boys say—every woman can be attractive. I'll admit that French girls come about as close to this as I've seen, I don't understand how. I see *Elle* and *Marie Claire* and *Paris Vogue* and I go to the French movies that play Toronto. As far as I can see, they're as chic as they care to be. They have those undernourished little figures though, which helps. We're all overfed.

I'm not small and piquant and thin-faced. I'm big, and even dieting I'm well-fed, and no amount of starvation will make my bones any smaller; you can't diet off wrists and collarbones and knees, and my father never let me get out of hand with dieting anyway.

"Now don't be silly, Marnie, 900 calories would make you unfit to have in the house, or in town."

"Oh, Dad."

"It strikes me that your Maker meant you to weigh about 135, and I don't think you'd be happy any lower."

"I'd be ecstatic at 110."

'That's being completely unrealistic. I'll write you out a simple easy 1900 calories per day which will keep you hovering around 132 or thereabouts. Paul wouldn't like you at 110."

"How can you tell?"

"Instinct. I would guess that Paul likes them monumental, like his buildings."

"Don't tease me."

"Listen, Marnie, a man who likes dolls is no bet for a husband. A man who likes them big is really looking for a woman, not a model, not a teenager. Be glad you're full-sized. I suppose it's hard to take."

"It's impossible to take."

"Ask him sometime, you'll see."

But you never give up hope that one fine morning you'll wake up looking like Marie-José Nat. I wonder what Paul

44

would think of that. It's true that he likes us big.

Though my darling duck loves a grown woman, I still insist that my rump is too big and slab-sided, and my upper arms are pretty fleshy on their underside, and in short I'm carrying about eighteen pounds too much here, and here, and there, Paul or no Paul. It's the nibbling that does it, and we know how that started, don't we? They'd fight all through dinner and I'd eat nothing, staring at my wobbly plate. "Oh she's picky!" And at ten that night I'd be standing in front of an open refrigerator, and now I'm carrying eighteen pounds of compulsion, but at least Paul likes it, bless his heart.

"Put him in the corner, he's left-handed. That's it, Paul, watch your elbow."

"That's Uncle Phil's place, Mother."

"Am I putting you out, Mr. McCredie?"

"No, no, boy, no, you're the guest of honour."

Dal McCruddy, grown now, and about to be an usher, leans across the table and leers at me. "Your fiianncy looks like the picture on the wall."

Mother naturally picks this up. "I thought so too." And she makes a general appeal to the company, her usual tactics. "Do you know what David did to me on our honeymoon?" She qualifies this with a terrible giggle, "I mean in the daytime."

"This is for Phil. Pass that along, will you, Dal?"

I'm sitting before a crack between leaves, as I have since babyhood. In the square window over the buffet the evening light thickens and dies; one star hangs in the window, a point of yellow gleam that I think is in my eye, and then identify as the first star, star bright. I wish to be good to Paul, and happy with him.

"He took me out to Devil Lake to fish and there was no water but what you carried in a huge pot from the shore; there was no plumbing of any kind, naturally, and flies at all times. It was simply awful. Do you want gravy, Dal?"

"Yeah, and could I have the celery? What are you kids going

45

to do?"

"We're going to the Film Festival."

"What Film Festival."

"Cannes. We can just work it in, on a 21-day excursion."

"Can," says Dal, "what do you want to go to Can for? There's a film festival in New York, I think."

"We thought we'd like to get out of the country for a while."

"Isn't this continent big enough for you?"

Mother laughs. "David took me to the outdoor plumbing festival, and Paul is taking Marnie to Cannes, difference between the generations. Is it that we're richer than our parents, or that our children have better taste than we?"

"Devil Lake is perfect, for what it is, Helen, and I never proposed it as anything but uncivilized. I simply misjudged you—I was a lot younger then. I don't know that I'd take you to Cannes, though, now that I can afford it. You wouldn't like it any better than Devil Lake; there'd be faults, and you'd find them. Will you give me some vegetables?"

She extends the gravy boat over his plate. "Where would you take me, what would I like?"

"No gravy, sweetheart. You like what you're doing. *This* is what you like." She floods his plate with gravy and it is silently handed down the table. Beige cheeks, tight collar, varnished skin, sandy-to-blond hair combed straight to either side of a widening part, slightly goitrous eyeballs. Paul is a dear, a dear, so kind. He winks at me across the table and nods at my plate, urging me to eat, and then turns and looks for an ashtray.

"Nobody minds? No room."

"Balance it on the keyboard." Dad hands him a Carling's Red Label ashtray and he sets it on the keys. The same treble chord that Uncle Phil struck for twenty summers tinkles in the close room.

"If you intend to smoke," says Mother, being tart to Paul for the first time, "open the door to the porch. Or, no, don't get up, Marnie, you can reach it." I rise and open the door, smel-

46

ling the fresh cut grass, thick on the lawn and all the way down the hillside. Now there are more stars, and there will be a multi-calorie dessert.

"Ladyfingers, by God," says Uncle Phil at my back, "haven't seen them in years."

"It's trifle, and you won't see that in Perth Amboy. Fruit cocktail, ladyfingers, brandy and whipped cream, all chilled."

"Christ, that's good."

Paul puts his arm around my waist and we stand in the door-way looking at the dark sky and sniffing the tedded grass; we bump hipbones; tomorrow night we'll be face to face. "Des-sert," he says, licking his full lips, and we go back and eat a great deal of the cold sweet mixture. After the dinner conver-sation the dessert silence is delicious.

I never met a man who didn't make me feel threatened with rape, they're all out for the same thing, men, they all look the same upside down, girls. Sexual folklore is full of disgust and instrumentalism. When I said I wasn't pretty I meant it, but any girl who isn't leprous or paralysed or otherwise incapable, who can open her legs, qualifies for the simple act, which is all most men care about. Upside down, it doesn't matter if you're pretty or not, you can provoke, and leave unsatisfied. I learned the signals from Ted Harasymchuk and others: some you will kiss on the third date, some you will kiss open-mouthed, some (fewer) are permitted to handle one breast, fewer both. And you never come across with the carrot until the donkey is in the stable.

Paul is getting rich, or will be shortly, and I'm only 24, see what a carrot buys you? According to Desmarais, Auchinleck, Papadopolous and Wise, he is the coming man, already a ju-nior and anonymous partner, his designs endorsed as those of the best young architect in the country. Did I marry him for his beautiful blueprints and his Utopian views or because he isn't a sexual threat.

"All young architects are virgins, they have the psychology of virgins before the event." Harasymchuk used to bait Paul terribly when we double-dated.

"Virgins?"

"You have high principles, you set a value on yourselves, you're going to improve the public lot." Paul and his pals always had some grandiose scheme for Toronto's rebirth with fountains, vistas, greenbelts and malls; they were great on malls. Turn a motorist into a pedestrian, they felt, and you've humanized a soul.

"I don't see what's so silly about that," Paul said, "architecture is queen of the arts, the only art that includes all the others."

Ted said: "Each of the arts makes that ridiculous claim."

"What about music?" I stuck this in to irritate him.

"Shut up, you," he said, "you're just an ignorant woman."

"You're a black Polack pig," I said, but he paid no attention.

"Ukranian," Paul said gently.

"It's all the same," I said, and that made Ted notice me.

"Ignorant bitch."

"All the arts take place in buildings," Paul said.

"Except those that take place outside." This stopped him in his tracks and he turned the conversation.

"Think what Toronto could be if we took some thought over it. Got the streetcar tracks off Queen Street, had pedestrian malls around City Hall, one of the world's great buildings."

"What is all this about pedestrian malls? Every time I talk to an architect he tells me what an evil thing an automobile is. If it weren't for automobiles, you'd be a farm boy guiding a plow in Haldimand County and I'd be a male whore in Minsk."

"What would I be?"

"Precisely what you are, a big dumb slob of a sleeping beauty with your brains in your bottom."

"Hit him, Paul," I said, but of course Paul only grinned.

"We ought to have a law cars couldn't come in any farther

48

than Eglinton. You could take the subway from there or use moving sidewalks."

Ted grimaced. "A law must be enforceable, if it is to be law."

"I may be a bit unrealistic. It's true."

"Why you aren't an artist at all; you're some ridiculous kind of social reformer like Ruskin or Morris, with your virginal high thinking. But the minute you get into somebody's office with a chance to earn some big dough you forget all about it. I know you guys, you can't face up to the way things are."

"And you're the one to tell us aren't you?" I said.

"I'm not interested in telling you anything. You make me sick, if you really want to know."

I said: "Nobody asked you to come sit at our table. Why don't you beat it, and leave us alone?" But after Ted went, Paul sat back and looked at me anxiously; he looked kind of varnished.

"Will I go bring him back?"

"Who, him? I wouldn't care if I never saw him again. He's a big nothing." I began to sniffle a bit.

"He shouldn't talk to people like that."

"No," I said, "he's a bully. He isn't gentle like you. Give me a kiss."

"What, here?"

"Take me home, then."

And so we were married, and so Desmarais, Auchinleck, Papadopolous and Wise give us the best of both worlds—money, and a feeling of cautious humanitarianism. Every other year Paul works on a new Juvenile Court or a master plan for the Toronto Parks Commission to keep in touch with the town-planners and their hot-eyed supporters, and in the meantime we have money, some, and more coming.

I'm not anti-money, and I hope to God the bottom drops out of the market for non-objectivist Toronto painters, that's all I hope. I never but once got through to a man, really through, and it wasn't somebody who threatened me with assault either.

49

I trusted my father. He never wanted to rape me, and we almost got to know each other, a near miss.

"I had a cut on my finger, a little cut. It could have been that."

"You really think so?"

"Perhaps. These things are transmissible, though not freely, and I've always been careful."

"Why liver trouble? I always thought that was for alcoholics. You're awfully brown, Dad."

"Ummmmm. The liver is strongly self-regenerative, you know."

"Oh, you'll be okay."

"Or it might have been developing fluid."

"You're kidding. That couldn't hurt you, could it?"

"As a matter of fact it can. A lot of these things have turned out to be pretty toxic. I read up a case some time ago of a boy who slept overnight in a sleeping bag that had just been dry-cleaned, and they couldn't wake him in the morning; he had inhaled too much. You've got to watch carbon tet, and apparently my darkroom is pretty poorly ventilated, something I'd never considered, or perhaps I wouldn't be here."

"That got at your liver?"

"So they believe. We're having a look to make certain. The hepatitis will go away in time, now that we've pinpointed the source, or will have, after tomorrow."

"Are you tired?"

"I tire easily. It goes with it, but don't leave for a minute. Tell me, how's Paul?"

"Great. He's down in the canteen with Mother; they're as thick as. . . well, not exactly thieves."

"You're lucky. I like Paul, he's very pleasant and obliging. I expect he's very good at what he does; those agreeable diffident men often are."

"He has good ideas. He'll probably do some designs for Ontario Place."

"Marnie, are you and Paul getting along? You know."

The hospital in Kingston is near the lakefront and you can see the water, canoeists and their girls, parasols, like an aquatic gala. It makes me remember the time Mimsy and I sank in the middle of the regatta course. "What did you say, Dad? I'm sorry, I missed it."

"Id like to do something for you if I could, to retrieve some of the damage I've done."

"Don't sit up, I'm leaving in a second. What damage?"

He makes a pitiable effort. "Listen to me, Marnie, because it might do you a lot of good. I want you to remember something. I want you to believe—you *must* believe—that no proper man will assault you or abuse you. Believe this, and don't be afraid."

"I believe it."

"Do so, then, and don't forget it."

We looked straight at each other and for once, for once, I got through the screen of another person's looks to the identity beyond. I really felt, as you feel moving water or an electric shock, the living movement of someone else's person. The only time. I knew him, and he gave me the freedom of the kingdom of men.

Move the piano out of the living-room, boys, and take the leaves from the table. Shorten it, and move it over there against the wall. Say hello to Lieutenant Dunglas, won't you? He'd be hurt. There we go, that's it, make room, because he'll be in here until the actual ceremony. What do you mean, it won't go through the door? It has to go through the door; it came in here 35 years ago by that door, and out it goes, the same way. Don't strike chords with your heedless elbows, just get it out of here. Shut all the doors, cut off the telephone, slide it along. We have to make room for the flowers and the benches and the candles. So much more, so infinitely more dignified, than going to a funeral parlour. I was married from here, I'll bury my father from here. Now where's that photo, ah, there. I don't like the frame but it's a good likeness. We'll have him up here beside the hero of the War of 1812. Pictures on the wall. Not to be afraid. Where's the hammer, is that good and straight?

What's that thing, looks like a sawhorse? Oh. Oh, of course. The flowers will be banked here, and the prie-dieu goes here, so I guess that goes across that, so, just so. Take a look at this picture will you, boys, does it look straight to you? Up a bit on this side? How's that? Good, we'll leave it like that. My friends, my gallery, these are not men but pictures. Men you have to touch.

Incendiaries

Married under a year, Tanse and George Marshland lost their first child at delivery. The pregnancy had been uneventful, regular, and Tanse hadn't felt sick in any way. She had golfed, done some riding, kept up the apartment, done nothing to effect such an accident.

It was a breech birth, hopelessly complicated by the premature emergence of the cord. Everything happened so fast at the end that Tanse never made it into the delivery room, which seemed odd. The nursing team hadn't quite known how to react. Harold Stepney, Tanse's obstetrician as well as a personal friend, just barely arrived in time to observe the death. As he came in the door he was hastily getting into a blue-green surgical coat and twitching the shoulders into place. Tanse could visualize the look of dismay on his face for months afterward. She was even able to tell him, at a cocktail party many weeks later, that he had had two drops of coffee in the corner of his mouth, caught in one of his laugh-lines; certain details had lodged vividly in her imagination as she was passing out.

She distinctly remembered that as poor little Ann Caroline came out of her body one of the friendliest of the nurses caught the child like a football and, sprinkling water on her forehead, baptized her. She lived for approximately four minutes but her brain tissue, respiratory system and heart action had been ruined by prolonged anoxia; there was never any question of her surviving.

Tanse knew from the moment of delivery that Ann Caroline had died. She said to herself that she'd always expected as

53

much, then went into her post-operative sedation with the ful-filled expectation stuck in her mind.

George didn't find out till sometime later. He'd gone to work that morning, unwilling to make a spectacle of himself around the hospital. From time to time during the day he checked in at the switchboard, and at 5 pm was told that Tanse had gone into heavy labour. They would keep him abreast of developments. When the baby died, at 6.04, he was putting a couple of pork chops into the broiler, whistling to himself and waiting for a call. By 7 o'clock he started to wonder why it didn't come. When he finally contacted the Maternity floor, they got Harold Stepney for him. Hal gave him the news as kindly as possible.

George went right over to Saint Dominic's, not wanting to make trouble—what could he do, after all—but dazedly ima-gining there might still be something he could arrange—a way to make things work out all right. He wasn't taking too much in. He talked to Hal and to Doctor Oelbaum, who had been pencilled in as their pediatrician.

"What happened?"

Oelbaum looked at his shoes. "It's a good thing she didn't live, smashed up like that. She might have had cerebral palsy. She might have been imbecilic. You're lucky in a way."

"I suppose so. What about Tanse?"

"She knows."

"Did she see it happen?"

"She was barely conscious. We're keeping her for several days, George," said Harold Stepney. "There's nothing wrong with Tanse, but it's better for everybody's peace of mind."

"I can see that."

"If you've prepared a room for the baby, take it apart before she comes home."

"Yes, thanks a lot, both of you." They went away. They had plenty on their minds. Harold Stepney had delivered 50 babies that month.

54

Tanse was in post-operative a long time; this made George jumpy. When he asked about her, the nurses reassured him but time dragged. He imagined all sorts of calamities. Jesus, he thought, I hope they didn't lose her too. But of course she was fine when they finally let him see her. She talked inconsequentially, the ramblings of someone in a euphoric dream. Remembering that they all acted like that, coming out of it, he didn't feel too alarmed. In the two hours he sat with her, she had a single moment of vivid clarity. "The baby's dead, George."

"I know," he said, smiling at her. "Hal told me. It's just one of those things."

She said, "It was a girl. These things happen, George."

"That's correct, Tanse."

"It's nobody's fault."

He finally left the hospital, and went straight home. He wanted to get to bed early because he'd been up most of last night. Anyway, he thought, Tanse will get a good rest.

She stayed at St. Dominic's for ten days, taking it easy and turning things over in her mind. During a flying visit, Hal asked if she'd like to see one of the residents in psychiatry.

"What for, for goodness' sake?"

"People sometimes do, after an accident like yours."

"Don't be silly," she said, rather impatiently. "I'm not reproaching myself for a thing."

"Of course not."

"Nor you either. You've been wonderful, Hal."

"So have you. . ."

George was getting their apartment ready for her return. They had put a lot of money into infant furnishings—a large crib, an elaborate layette, toys adapted to all stages of baby's first years. They'd been given many presents, which he didn't know what to do with. Should he send them back? It wasn't like a broken engagement; it wasn't their fault. In the end he packed the presents and the toys into five large cartons and had a welfare agency pick them up. In a way, he was sorry to see them go; some of the toys were cute. He had had fun playing with one particular woolly duck.

He bought paint, and rolled it over the nursery wallpaper, thinking as he did so that he was going to extremes, feeling like a guilty character in a Victorian novel. They had taken six months to get all this junk together; it took him four days to get rid of it. He had no idea whether Tanse would be able to have another try.

When she came home there were no daytime-serial effects. They shared a certain hardihood, Tanse and George, which blurred the lines of what had happened. Looking at the situation objectively, they told each other, they had never known the baby and they wouldn't miss her as a person. The ZPG people would approve. They split a bottle of wine at dinner, played some favourite Dylan records and made plans.

"I'd figured fifteen hundred for child care the first six months. We aren't going to spend it," said George.

"There's a lot we could do instead."

"We could treat ourselves to a couple of plane tickets to Europe." The idea of just taking off and popping over for a couple of weeks struck them as pleasant, faintly glamorous. It was easy for George to get three weeks away from the plant; his status was high and everyone was very sympathetic. Their parents had sent them sizeable sums of money when they were expecting the baby, which they thought should be used to "take Tanse's mind off things."

Between themselves, they admitted that there was no special need to divert her; she was fine, just fine. But since an excuse to fly to Europe doesn't present itself every day, they snatched at the opportunity. They bought two of those dizzy sixteen-stopover things from SAS, flew to Prestwick and passed their vacation hopping from city to city, ending with Copenhagen which they thought overrated, certainly nothing to compare with Amsterdam. They had never been much grabbed by

Scandinavia anyway.

After they came back, the excitement wore off quickly, and soon they were on the lookout for some new amusement. George had his work, which was technical and demanding, and a piece of private research, with which he sometimes occupied himself at home in the evenings. But all Tanse had to do was manage the apartment, and this didn't seem enough. Golf and riding seemed pretty childish to her now; they were ephemeral, unworthy of adult attention. She kept up her housework conscientiously, moving furniture around continually, designing a room-divider, framing her own drawings. She went now and then to the smaller galleries looking for lithographs and silkscreens which would fit her decor. Sometimes she bought one, always on approval until she'd shown it to George.

He looked at the prints with earnest attention but little understanding. "It gives you something to do," he said once, insantly realizing that he'd been slightly tactless.

"It's just a hobby, George, like anything else."

"Do whatever you like," he would say generously. She had so much freedom that it was oppressive. When she suggested her notion of starting a collection of oils, he didn't laugh as he might have done when they were first married. He listened to her soberly.

"You know I'm not too well up on the local painters," he said. "But start buying, by all means, if it gives you pleasure. Get out and look around."

She looked and looked but never found what she wanted. She thought of having her portrait done, but rejected the idea as narcissistic. The simple truth, she saw, was that she hadn't enough responsibility. But what was there? The apartment. She had a lofty contempt for the petty politics, the nasty self-publicizing, that went with amateur social work. She was not the course-taking type. Many of her friends were up to here in political action, or the Civil Liberties Union, or a consciousness-raising group, or a women's drop-in centre. Their accounts of these activities, different in detail, displayed in general a fundamental aimlessness. She was so free. What was she to do?

In the middle of such thoughts she often found herself standing in the third bedroom, picking out the patterns in the nursery wallpaper under the thin layer of paint which George had considerately rolled on. At such times she had to shake herself to keep back tears.

"Self-love, self-pity," she said aloud one day, gritting her teeth angrily, staring at herself in the mirror in the third bedroom. That night she brought up her boredom and half-realized loneliness. It was true, she had found, that though she had never gotten to know Ann Caroline, she missed her.

"I wish that hadn't happened," she said.

"We'll get in touch with Harold Stepney," said George sensibly, "and we'll find out if it's all right to try again."

"I think that would be the best thing," she said gloomily.

Doctor Stepney gave her a thorough examination and a bit of a talking-to. "There's nothing the matter with you. There never was. The way you were carrying the baby was purely accidental, a million-to-one-shot. You can have a baby any time you care to try."

"You're really sure?"

"Look, you want one, don't you?"

"I do."

"Well, then. . ."

"Hal, is that all you've got to say?"

"Oh for goodness's sake, Tanse. Go home and do your best to get pregnant."

She followed the doctor's orders and enjoyed herself tremendously for several months, without any regard to consequences. In due course the Marshlands began to expect another child.

As soon as Tanse was sure, she began to burn with impatience. She and George began again the laborious process of collecting baby-furnishings; this time they knew better what to look for, and it didn't take as long. They evolved a second collection of toys, although there weren't as many contributions from friends and relatives. Having been taken in a first time, previous donors were no doubt more wary. Tanse took much pleasure in the toy-collection; she instructed George to find another woolly duck of the type he had enjoyed so much before. One night in her fifth month, they were sitting by the coffee table squeezing stuffed animals at each other, with a wide range of soft quacks and grunts, laughing quietly at their own babyishness, when she got another idea.

"We should have a pet for the baby, a puppy or a kitten. We could have it all trained by the time she arrives." They thought of the baby as "she" in mutual remembrance of the dead Ann Caroline. "Young children love pets," she asserted, fondling a toy bear.

"You don't think it would be cruel to keep one in an apartment?"

"If we can rear a baby in an apartment, we ought to be able to keep a little kitten."

"It's a kitten you want?"

"For the baby. . ."

"The baby, yeah. I've always liked kittens myself. I think that would be fun."

"Let's have one then."

"Fine."

They were too canny to consult a pet shop, understanding that such places rip off their customers for quite ordinary animals. Tanse had once owned a horse, and knew a thing or two about the upkeep of animals. Admittedly a horse and a kitten were two very different items. A horse was almost as bad as a sailboat as far as upkeep went; she had been greatly relieved to be rid of Cavort, handsome though he had certainly been.

"Remember that damned horse?" said George, while they tried to think of a place to get a kitten reasonably; they didn't want just an alley-kitten.

"Cavort? My God, George, don't remind me."

"I wonder what he's doing now?"

"Eating."

"Yes, I guess so. What about this kitten, Tanse?"

"I believe I'll give Polly a call; she has cats; she'll know."

Polly Ziegler was a tough, pretty, rich girl who had been at Miss Hill's with Tanse. Many people disliked her because of her impenetrably polished exterior. Tanse, who could recall when they had wailed together over their orthodontia, was less put down by this surface than most; all you had to do was to tell Polly to go to hell now and then. She might be rich but she didn't belong on any pedestal.

"Let me put you straight," said Polly crisply, over the phone. "You don't want to get involved with the cat-fanciers. They're all Lesbian or crazy. Stay away from cats with impressive papers."

"We just want a good-looking pet for the baby."

"Tell you what you do. There's a woman who lives near Jay Peak, who disposes of superfluous kittens for people as a kind of private humane society. Why don't you run down and see her? I'll tell her you're coming. You might pick up a fine specimen for $10." She told Tanse how to find the place; it was a real farm and everything.

"Thanks very much, Polly."

"No trouble! Oh, and leave high-priced pairs of Siamese alone. I keep finding mine riding round and round in the dryer." She snorted abruptly and hung up.

On Saturday George and Tanse took a run down to Vermont, where they located the cat hostel easily. The proprietress, who turned out somewhat disconcertingly to be a very chic gentlewoman-farmer, a monied pal of Polly's, gave them their choice of half a dozen cute little fluffballs. They wanted a male, but George was so won over by an indeterminate little thing that fastened its claws in his sweater that they took it without settling the mystery of its sex.

He or she didn't seem to feel strange at all, but scampered

60

all over the living-room as soon as they got home. They felt so good about their acquisition that George decided they'd have a little party with wine, pickles, shrimp, the works. He went to the delicatessen, always a sign of impending extravagance, where he made many exotic purchases, including a can of rattlesnake meat for the kitten, and a jar of guava jelly for the Melba toast. Meanwhile Tanse set the table with their best china and her heirloom candlesticks. When George got back, they put *The Magic Flute* on the stereo, lit the candles, and sat down to a huge and rather silly meal of cold canned Scotch pheasant, much wine, and brandy with the coffee. They passed their new pet back and forth, admiring its fluffy, silky fur.

"I think it's going to be a longhair," said Tanse, pleased.

"Aren't they usually thoroughbreds?"

"Yes, usually, at least I think so. She said this was a Maine coon cat. Isn't he—or she—an active little thing? What'll we call him? Her?" Setting the kitten on the coffee table in front of her, she picked up her brandy and took a ceremonial swallow.

The kitten's claws scratched comically on the polished table as he moved carefully toward George, picking his way delicately through the dishes and bottles. Suddenly his small legs slid out from beneath him and he bumped against a candlestick. As they watched, in trance-like slow motion, the candle fell on the kitten and set its fur on fire.

They could hear a bass voice on the stereo singing *In Diesen Heil'gen Hallen.*

The fine fur blazed up in shocking brightness as they sat there watching; then there was a singed smell and the animal cried horribly. It jumped from the table and began to run crazily around the room. They still didn't move. The smell changed; the flesh was being seared.

"George!" she shouted, breaking the spell, and he leaped to his feet, picked up a cushion, saw that it was useless, and ran to the nearest bedroom for a blanket. When he came back, the

61

kitten was still running, slower now, and he had trouble getting his hands on it. Finally he threw the blanket over it and the cries stopped. He rolled the blanket up and held it, feeling heat in his hands. They waited for several minutes.

When he unrolled the blanket, they saw that it was no good. Whether it had died of burns or shock, or had been smothered, they couldn't tell. George stood up. Tanse stared at him, her thickening body trembling with nervous reaction, her eyes round with horror and flowing with tears.

"Whose fault was that?" she sobbed. "Who's to blame?" He was frightened by her look. She cried again, "Oh, whose fault is it this time?"

Thanksgiving: Between Junetown and Caintown

Certainly those places exist, go look them up! Do you suppose I've imagined this?

So does Blue Mountain. It sticks up on the south shore like a nubbin, a nipple, a giant woman's breast. The skyline runs along, not very high above the water, then there's this—what should I say—this protruberance. I don't like to speak frivolously of my own sex, and our sexual parts. All the same, Blue Mountain is shaped like a tit. I can't explain what I might have been doing, climbing up it like a flea on the breast of a goddess, but there we were. "Three and a half hours going and coming." I don't know where he gets his information. "Who told you that, how do you know, are you sure? I have other things to do. I want to cut some corn stalks and draw them."

"Ron told me."

He has this—this really *pathetic*—dependence on what people tell him.

"Well naturally if Ron told you then it must be true, I mean Ron knows everything."

"He knows the lake; he's lived here all his life."

"Three and a half hours?"

"So he says."

"I've always wanted to go, actually, and the leaves are marvellous this weekend, and we won't be back before spring."

"And there'd be the flies in the spring."

"Got it all figured out, haven't you? Did Ron tell you that?"

"We won't get bitten even once," he said, bounding joyfully on ahead, incurably hopeful, eager to placate when there is nobody to please, to mollify, no wrong to expiate. He cannot realize that it is exactly his folly that I love; he is so ready to adventure.

We drove along in early afternoon in unbelievable sunshine under skies of unmixed clarity. I don't believe in auguries. Clear skies are mere atmospheric conditions, smog the effect of miscalculation. You will not catch me prancing through meadows, nor does my heart lift at a soft breeze. What I want is an access road to hard reality. I am a dreadful mean woman. I am.

He knew just where to go, up a foul side road with deep pools of muddy water every 50 feet. "Bit of a dip here, hum hum." We drove due north, and I will allow that the lie of the land was lovely, the way it sloped. I thought of snowmobiles and terrified small animals. We left the car on this awful cart track at 1.30.

I said, "Turn it around."

"What?"

"Here's a wide space in the road, we'll be tired and ready to go when we come down, why not turn it around?"

"Good thinking."

He does drive well, and he knows where things are after he asks around. "This fence is the border between Lansdowne and Escott, and the road back there was the fifth concession. Don't you want to hear?"

"No."

"Come on, it's interesting. This here was originally the Austin lot, and over there was all Websters, and they're all still here."

"Dead and buried."

"Darling, we're all dead and buried in the long run."

Hard reality clothed in endearment, perhaps that is the essence of marriage, anyway it was what I got from him on this sunny Sunday on Thanksgiving weekend, and it will have to do me till we finally get somewhere.

64

I felt the rise in the height of land pulling in my legs, each step forward an infinitesimal lift, the foot in an appreciably higher position than before. A man looking like a scoutmaster swung past us, hurrying along, calling out distances and botanical observations to the four children who followed him— his own children evidently, out for a pleasant afternoon climb. They moved fast, but we kept them in sight. Sometimes one of the children lagged behind his father to give us a lead. Eventually they passed along up ahead.

"We can follow the Hydro line."

"I don't see any Hydro line."

"But there is one. It goes right to the top. I guess they must have run in a power line for the logging; there's a logging road comes up from the lakeshore."

"I don't see it."

"It's good to know it's there."

It wasn't there. It doesn't exist. Nobody ever used electric power on top of Blue Mountain; they chopped down trees the way they did everywhere else, by brute force, using their arm muscles. And come to that, they never did much logging up there; the brush is uncut first-growth. We passed upward from the fields into this fuzz; then it thickened and the ground rose sharply. I began to pant. I take very small steps and I detest physical exertion. I'm not young. I'm getting fat. We climbed through closer woods over great rocky humps, keeping the sun on our left. My woodsman, my model of crafty lore, he kept hollering cheerfully that the sun was on our left hand, as if he'd invented it. We started to hear cries in the woods from all directions. I noticed that it was hard to tell where they came from; they appeared to move around. A voice might seem to come from up ahead, off to the right, then suddenly move around behind you. This could have been the effect of wind; more likely it was because of these gullies and creek beds we kept crossing. The ground didn't rise gently and gradually, as it had lower down. Voices multiplied. Somewhere nearby there was a crowd, or crowds, hikers, weekenders. We had been climbing for over an hour now and were close to the final rise. It made me think of the ascent of Kanchenjunga or Everest. Base camp at the 27,000-foot level. The final gallant attempt at the summit. Loyal Sherpas. Frozen bodies lowered, sewn in canvas sacks and lashed to sleds, from icy immolation on the roof of the world.

Blue Mountain is 700 feet high. A little bit of a hill, what a fuss over nothing. All the same there were things to see. Around three o'clock we came out of thick woods into swamp, an arm of a blocked creek, and the biggest beaver dam you ever saw. Made a little lake over drowned swampland with hundreds of spiny bare unleaved narrow tree trunks standing up dead. A squirrel's nest in every third tree. They must scamper around in the air like circus aerialists on a lace of shivering dead branches. They'd never have to come down to earth; they may live up there.

That dam must be 40 feet across, curved, looking like the work of human hands, engineers. We stepped along the rim making deep soggy footprints along the edge and ruining our shoes. It was hard to get across, but I liked seeing such a place.

After that we were well away, only had to cross another gully, a very deep one, silent, way down in shadow out of the reach of the sun. I could see rays of light striking the tops of trees, and the final hump of rock up ahead, but where we were was dark and still. Many of the trees had shredded lengths of red plastic tied to them, trail markers, used because red plastic doesn't react with anything. When you swallow it, your liver rejects it and it may lodge in your organs permanently. Nothing alters it, not bile, not snow, not sun. When beavers eat it, they die. This is not the material I'd pick for blazing trails. But it lasts forever. When this wilderness has been cut over and destroyed ages in the future, those bits of red plastic will be on the spot, fluttering in an arid wind.

We had to move from right to left and back, casting around

for the best place to make our move to the top. Coming right at it, you have to make the difficult ascent up the sheer face. There I go, making like Sir Edmund Hillary, but there really is a sheer face maybe 30 feet high and not sheer in the sense of being at a right angle with the ground. Seventy degrees perhaps, sheer, but not sheerness absolute. At this point we were in sunlight again and had gotten above the tops of the trees. We were beginning to get a view, and what a view! Worth it? I can't answer that; what can you do with a view?

Finally we were balanced on a hump of rock looking up at this 30-foot climb. My man hates heights, so now he let me take the lead. "I made an error," he said, "I looked behind me."

"You shouldn't have done that."

"I ought to have kept my nose flat against the rock. It's the eye focus, you see. It isn't fear of falling exactly. It's something in the eye muscles that frightens me when they move. You don't know what it's like. It's paralyzing."

I looked at the rock. There was a fissure in it eighteen inches wide, enough to jam a foot in for support, then the other, and so up to the top. You had to cuddle in against the face; you couldn't manage where there was overhang.

"I'll go first."

"I wish you would."

"Well I will."

He hung back. He thinks he's a coward. He has no notion what I think. I've seen him overcome various fears and I respect that. A phobia—heights, cats, confined spaces—you're not responsible. A phobia doesn't mean you're a coward. I'm not bothered by heights but I didn't earn the immunity so I don't feel superior, but I can't convince him. Perhaps it's good for him to think that I think he's a coward; it might spur him on.

I started up this fissure and it was easy as long as you didn't mind openness and the long view. I could feel my rear end looming over other climbers and blocking out the sun. I stuck out. I felt awkward. Grace is impossible under pressure of physical laws. I protruded, gritted my teeth and arrived on top of Blue Mountain and oh, I have to admit, the view!

I called down to where he waited, "Stay there for a few minutes." He smiled. He doesn't sulk. I left him then and crossed the top of the hill and fell over a couple who'd come there to make love. Solitary in the wilderness, concealed from prying eyes by three hard miles of tangle and obscurity, they'd wanted to embrace, to be united, say simply to love, and here I came, fat, clumsy, making excuses, a jolt for passion. "I'm so sorry, I had no idea, do please excuse me, I'll go away, actually I'm looking for a place for my husband to get up. He can't make it." They glared at me, thinking I might be ridiculing them by oblique references to male powerlessness. I passed on, coming finally to a cairn and cleared space facing north.

It was like taking a huge blown-up map of the lake and squinting at it on its edge instead of looking down at it. You saw it all in wide-angle perspective: Ron's place at the creek mouth miles and miles away, the Landing, the Outlet, the five wide reaches lying open like fingers of an almighty hand, Big Water, Deep Water, Running Bay, Webster Bay, Donaldson Bay, thirteen miles across, all lying out there with close unbroken bush falling away in front of me to the shore, no logging road, no power line, primordial.

I became aware of whoopings and rejoicings, Swarms of people appeared behind me carrying cases of Molsons, decks of cards, blankets. I thought of the isolated lovers and wanted to laugh. People crowded around makeshift fireplaces, and soon the smell of charcoal and burnt hot dogs rose up.

"They bussed us out to the Junetown four corners."

"Up the eastern trail."

"Trail?"

"50 of us. Young Anglicans."

"Is there an easy way to get up from there?"

"Right over there, lady."

"I've got my husband, you see."

"Haven't we all, haw haw haw."

I pushed through the gaping throng—must have been 70 of them. Children. In this mountain fastness. I heard a baby wailing in a papoose pack. A man lurched up and said, "I'm Toby O'Grady. I went to school with your father." He held a beer bottle. How had he managed the climb? Did he perhaps dwell here, the attendant spirit of the mountaintop, an Ontario Jove?

I got back to the edge and looked down and spotted him, the poor thing, sitting by himself. I don't know if he'd heard the merry throng above, hidden from him like the angels. I got his attention.

"Hey, come along to your right, it isn't more than a hundred yards."

"But a hard hundred yards."

"Push through the junipers and be careful where you put your feet." In the end he wandered around in the sunshine to the east end of the spur leading to the top, and came up what was almost a path, surprised by the ease of the ascent, put off by the crowd. He's always hidden back in there, doesn't believe I know how far. So cheerfully withdrawn. "Look at them all."

"Come on up, it won't bother you."

"No, I'm not bothered by a wide open space on flat ground. Look what you can see! I've been wanting to do this for years."

I stood off and watched him and thought about personal incapacity. Things we will not do, things we cannot, spaces, lacks in us. He can't take height. All his actions are worked around this incapacity—driving miles to avoid a high bridge, imposing a special condition upon the possibilities of life, how this must hurt, excise, make impossible, close off ranges of action. And we all do this. I do it. I am aware what I cannot, will not, do. Some things you can't; some you won't; some you neither can nor will, and these terminate, finish, kill, end, oh, oh.

Picnics still going on with laughter.

"Let's go down."

"Sure."

Already young Anglicans were setting out for Junetown, four miles southeast. They trotted by in clumps, sinking suddenly down into dark on an unfamiliar path, moving quickly. The sun was getting over toward the Outlet and seemed more to the north than when we came up. I guess it was close onto four, maybe five to four, when we started down, and by four o'clock we were alone, the Junetown hikers disappeared, their noises dispersed, now seeming to come from all around, then receding into stillness.

He said softly, "We should be on the other side of that spur."

The sun was at our backs.

"What do you mean?"

"I never came up this way. I came up the other side. We should be on the other side of that spur. I crossed it just about here."

My trouble was that I hadn't been watching when he came up. I'd taken no note.

"It was here. I crossed here."

"All right, so let's go. We'll go back down along the hump, past where you couldn't make it to the big beaver dam and along down."

"Right."

We went along in silence for five minutes, eight minutes. I knew I'd never seen any of this before. I have no sense of direction. He went on ahead. We came off a ridge and when I looked back I couldn't see the top of the mountain, just a lot of anonymous brush. I trailed him into a swampy tract that suddenly got much too deep, grabbing at our knees.

"Hey, Hey!"

"What is it?"

"Do you know where we are? Did you come through this?"

"No."

70

"Are we lost?"

"Let's go on a bit. The beaver dam should be right over there." He gestured vaguely.

At 4.15 we got down into deep shadow. I thought, it will be dark by six, the second weekend in October. Last night was cold in the cottage. We have to be back at the car before dark. I said, "I don't think we're doing the right thing." It stopped him in his tracks and he turned and looked at me. On his face was an expression I'd never seen and didn't understand.

He said, "Right now we're lost." What struck me was how completely quiet the woods were, not a sound from hikers or lovers, yet they couldn't be more than a mile off. You can be utterly lost in a square mile of heavy cover; you can freeze listening to the sound of motor horns, helicopters, searchers. He began to shout, "Helllooooo," every few seconds. I thought he'd drive me mad. Nobody answered and there was no echo. Time passing. It had taken us two hours to climb up, and it was 4.30. It would be completely dark at 6.30.

I thought: here it is then. I stood on ground I'd never seen in my life, and had no idea in the world how to get back. These gullies ran round and round the side of the hill; you could circle in them and never come down. I thought: don't twist your ankle, don't move too suddenly over rock, you couldn't crawl out. I looked at my husband. I knew he wasn't a coward. I'd always trusted him. We were lost. Good and lost. I, who had never been afraid of anything in my life, thought about dying here. This fear got swiftly worse for fifteen minutes. In a quarter of an hour we got the whole local experience in concentrated form, heady stuff.

"We have to go back to the top and start again."

"I don't think we can find it." I was sorry as soon as I'd said this. I didn't like the way his face went. He cried out again and again, "Helllooooo." I thought of a lost child crying for its mother. I'd have cried out for help myself, but who to?

"Which way is up?"

"Come on," he said, and he led me back through the swamp. "If we keep climbing up toward the sun, we'll be back on top in fifteen minutes. Then we can get our bearings. We know we have to go due south. If we walk straight south for two hours, we'll have it made. We'll be doing just the reverse of what we did coming up." He babbled on. I paid no attention. What could I do? I followed along and thought: building a shelter. How build? We have a penknife. But no food. No matches. No compass. No flashlight. Last night it was cold; we had the stove on, then the heater, then we lit a coal fire. Don't sprain an ankle.

I thought we might last one night if we had to and tomorrow would be Thanksgiving. If the weather was fair, other hikers might come up. If we could go through a night. How do you make a shelter?

"Hey, there it is."

I looked up, and he was right, we'd got back on top, at least there was nowhere higher to climb. It didn't look exactly like where we'd been earlier, but the view was the same. We could spot our neighbour's boat ramp at fifteen miles. My knees shook.

"Look," he said, pulling aside junipers.

"What?"

"Fencing down. A fence."

Late afternoon, sun well down. I was starting to cry. I wouldn't cry in front of him. I would not. I said, "We're three miles up, over bad ground. Can we get down before dark? We'd have to follow the fence hand over hand in the dark."

"It tells us where men have been before. Look, the posts. If somebody planted those posts, we can follow their line and go out. It'll take time."

He kissed me on the forehead. I didn't touch him. "Let's not waste time."

"No."

We had an hour and a half till dark and a line to follow,

sometimes interrupted, sometimes lying under heaped-up leaf mold or running through heavy juniper. Once I sat down abruptly from a height of four feet onto a boulder-edge, and bruised a square foot of my hip. When the fence line broke he would turn and say, "Stick right on this spot and watch that I'm keeping in line. If I get out of sight, keep calling out so I can come straight back. I won't go any farther than I know I can retrace." Oh, he was full of ideas. I noticed that he'd stopped calling out and it made me feel better. I began to see that we'd be all right even if we had to spend the hours of darkness here; we could go on walking at daybreak. My hip hurt. My feet were blistered. Here he was, back again.

"I've found the next bit of fence on the other side of this gully. Careful now, stay in line. It ends with this big tree, stay in line till we get to the other side of the break." Full of advice.

"I heard a car horn."

"Yeah, figures. We can't be more than two miles from the road. I wonder if anybody will remember about us, if we don't pick up the car before dark."

"It will be interesting to see." I was puzzled why the sun had moved so far to the north, then terribly frightened again when the fenceline stopped for good. I heard him crashing around in front of me, down a creek bed and up the other side. We kept calling back and forth. "Does it stop for good?" "I can't find it; the line's broken." "What'll we do? Can we keep straight south without it?" "Can you find your way to me, no, wait, don't move, don't leave that end of the fence till we figure this out." "Oh, I heard calling. I heard a train." "Me too, we can't be too far off it now. Hold it, don't move away from the wire. I think I can see some clear space, look off to your left toward the southeast."

"How do you know it's the southeast?"

"I think we've been going southeast without knowing it. And I do see breaks in the trees. So now, watch out, don't lose your line, just come away from the end of the fence and down

73

into the creek. You should see stepping stones in black mud at the low point. Got it?"

Taking directions from him! "Yes, yes, yes, now I see you. I'm coming up. You're right, it is clearing." We stumbled on and in ten minutes, around six o'clock, he slipped in a patch of cow dung. "We're in somebody's back pasture, we're all right now, they'd never let their cattle wander too far away."

It was rocky upland, but cleared, studded with harsh out-croppings, farthest back pasture, welcome sight, with the ruins of a barn and the stones of what had been a cellar set in the middle of the field, with the very faint impression of wagon wheels running away to a chained gate. In the next field were living creatures, cows. Oh happy happy cows, I thought. The light was coming down mighty grey. We came to a road in near-twilight, not the same road we'd started out on.

"We're miles from the car," I said.

"Yeah. We're way over east around the Junetown inter-section."

"Oh how do you know."

"I've been up this road once before looking for the moun-tain."

"When, if you're so smart?"

"Once, once."

We straggled on down this stony track.

"In a while we'll come to a pig farm by a crossroads."

Damn it, he was right. About half past six we came out to this crossroads and sighted a white house, stucco over logs, along a dim grey road in the very last twilight. At the four corners was a stinking square of fenced dirt. Through the gloom I saw an enormous boar glaring at me balefully. He had the biggest testicles I've ever seen, swollen sore-looking grey hemispheres, and made threatening noises, moving to-ward us.

"This is Junetown."

"*This?* This is nothing."

74

"There was a settlement here in the old days, and Caintown is along the road. Let's go and beg a lift back to the car."

We went along the Caintown road to the farmhouse drive and so up to the house. In the kitchen four persons were preparing a holiday dinner of roast goose and a lot of wine: a schoolteacher from Lansdowne, a chemistry demonstrator from the city, two bearded musicians, civilization. The chemistry demonstrator drove us five miles in pitch dark west along unmarked back roads to where an oblong dark box lay next to a mudhole, our car. He waved goodbye and drove away to his goose and wine. It was seven pm.

"I'll drive," he said, "shall I? Will I drive then?"

I had nothing to say. I said nothing.

The Chess Match

Getting up in the morning, Mr. Page Calverly deferred as long as possible his first look in the mirror; that one must shave with the greatest of particular caution was unquestionable, for the sake of decency and dignity. The confrontation of the mirror was inescapable. It could however be put off for some minutes, those first aching minutes of wakefulness after the strange sleep that he nowadays endured.

He had noticed increasingly in the last decade or so that the metaphors for sleep were all young men's metaphors. Macbeth was plainly a young man, certainly not over 60, if he still considered sleep the balm of hurt minds. As for Keats, thought Mr. Calverly, his notion of sleep was infantile. No poet had dealt truly with the sleep of the very old, so unlike the easy drift of the metaphors, the comforting warm blanket, the total oblivion.

His own sleep was a horrid parody of wakefulness. He had no dreams. He lay in his expensive bed on the firmest of mattresses, guaranteed against morning backache, and felt aches in his back perpetually, and stiffenings and unstiffenings of his muscle-strings, and leaps of his heart, pauses in his respiration, sudden sweats, awful black seconds of unconsciousness which frightened him terribly, though not to death—never to death —nervous tics—he couldn't think and he couldn't forget his situation and the plain fact that his situation couldn't be eased or altered. When you are 86 years old, your situation is susceptible of no easement but the last.

He had never been an anti-clerical, despising the attitude as adolescent; but the sight of priests frightened and repelled him these days; they looked like crows or blackbirds.

Waking was merciful; here was another day to get through, an unexpected dividend, something he had no right at his age to expect, and he felt every morning an urge that he'd expected for years to lose, the impulse to rise, shake off his fears and the corollaries of his unalterable situation, and go about in this man's world as the equal of anybody. He rolled unsteadily out of bed and stood erect, putting a shaking finger to his eye and flicking out of its corner a ball of dried tears.

It was all still here for another day: the world, the streets, his place in the world, his neat small apartment which he paid for, nobody else, which was cleaned and aired weekly by a woman whom he hired and paid, who used his vacuum-cleaner and floor-polisher. He felt a kind of pride, which bothered him —it was almost senile—in his appliances, in the idea that a man born in 1890 should even have heard of such things as floor-polishers. He had visited old folks' homes now and then and the smell of those places had taught him, if nothing else, that floor-wax smelled like perfume, when you compared it to some other smells. His neat little place smelled of floor-wax and furniture polish, and his wardrobe smelled like a laundry, all starch and clean linen, paid for by him, and not of old men's urine, spittoons, unaired beds and lilies.

He had been away from the office now for 21 years, as long as a young man's minority. He had been a stockbroker with seats on the New York and Toronto exchanges, and when he had sold out for the last time he had taken enough money with him to last him out a good while. He had never touched his capital, which provided him with a snug income not much affected by the decline in the value of the dollar. The articles he bought hadn't increased that sharply in price, so that in 1976 his snug income served him almost as well as it had in 1955. At that time the size of his income had made him definitely well-to-do and there had even been some question of his

77

squiring widows about town. He had tried this once or twice before he was seventy.

These days he was still almost, not quite, to be described as well-to-do. "Comfortable" was nearer the mark. The single advantage that he had discovered in advanced age was the sensible diminution of one's wants. He no longer bought books, couldn't read them with any facility, and anyway he already had books. He bought no more sheet music since his fingers had grown so stiff, the piano was silent. Records mocked his hearing; the best of them sounded like the distorted scratchings he remembered from his young manhood. And yet, he had heard, the new records were extraordinarily lifelike. When he spoke to someone it was apt to be on the subject of the new recordings, which he discussed with easy familiarity although he had never really heard the stereophonic effect as it must sound to those who can hear properly.

What did he do? He kept up his end of the game. He bathed —for of course he daren't attempt a shower—scrubbing himself meticulously. It took him a long time. There are no metaphors for the physical feelings of the aged. A young man says that he feels weak, and he means that his normal strength is somewhat dissipated. Mr. Calverly was weaker all the time than one can describe—there are no standards for comparison. Johnny has a nervous tremor of the hands when he applies for a job. Mr. Calverly was, figuratively speaking, applying for that job every second of the day. His hands shook perpetually, keeping him from extending them in the normal masculine greeting, except when he felt very well indeed which was not often. It was a downright embarrassment to him to have to shake hands.

He was infrequently embarrassed; he made no new friends.

When he had bathed, trying to keep out of his mind the disgust he felt as he examined his narrow legs, the legs of some prisoner of the concentration camps, the belly of a starved man, when he had warmed himself with the hot water and scented himself with soap, he let the water drain from the tub, down to the very last drop. Then he mopped out the tub as he sat there, determined to avoid a wrenching slip or a fall, and, placing his old feet as solidly as he could on the rubber mat in the tub, he climbed laboriously out and as laboriously stood up. He had been a tall man and though he had shrunk a full two inches he was still nearly erect. Each morning after his bath he drew himself as straight as he could, pulled his shoulders back, inflated his chest, slipped his denture into his mouth and gripped shakily at it with his gums. The denture altered the entire aspect of his face, filled it out, changed it from a grotesque to a recognisable caricature. Then he faced the mirror.

What did he see? He only saw what we all see or will see, his face, himself, what else is there to see? It was still the only face of Page Calverly and could have been that of no-one else. The face that had looked back at him since he had used mirrors, how long? It was his own face, the bones were there, the same slight peculiar angle to the cheek bones that had made him attractive to young women at Varsity in the reign of Edward VII. If any of those young women had been alive to tell, they would have put his name to that face at once. There was the plane of the upper lip which belonged also to his father, born in 1864, and his grandfather, born just after the Congress of Vienna, who had talked of Wellington and Peel as the most active of his contemporaries. Mr. Calverly remembered that same long upper lip in a miniature of his grandfather which had been lost, how long ago?

He shaved with every conceivable accuracy though his hands shook almost uncontrollably, and he thanked God as he did every day for the invention of the safety razor. He had long ago determined that there should be no patches of missed bristles hiding in the deep wrinkles that furrowed the skin below his cheek bones. Whatever else happened he meant to keep his person immaculate as long as he could.

As he worked his razor into the folds and corners of his face, he studied the reflection before him, the old face like a shrunken apple, the papery grey skin. He still had much of his hair, grey hair, not white, and he combed and arranged it carefully. He had realized—oh, it must be twenty years ago—that one was not obliged to wear the uniform of the aged if one had money. Why do the old wear those club-like sloppy broken shoes and those hideous lavender dresses and rusty suits? He had decided to wear, not young men's clothes—he didn't want to appear ridiculous—but clothes that any grown man might wear without seeming to ape the fashions of youth.

The reason why old people wear those awful, unbecoming, dirty and worn clothes, is that they have no money. It isn't that they are pleased with them, or positively wish to stress the unpleasantness of their condition; but they are trapped, on the shelf, pushed into the corner with scarcely money to feed themselves, with none for pretty or handsome clothes, for decent haircuts and hairdressing, for laundry, manicuring, extra calories, even for razor blades sharp enough to give a decent shave.

Mr. Calverly prided himself on a peculiar discovery of his own; he had decided that he and a few others like him were the first old people in history, excluding the very rich and the aristocracy, to possess means sufficient to dismiss forever the ravages which old age had always previously worked upon the personal appearance.

It wasn't, he had worked out with himself, that one's appearance was the beginning and end of life, even at his age. But those others, the incomprehensible young, wouldn't treat you with their customary contumely if they saw that you were still able to care for your appearance. He meant not to be shelved, not to be put away in the corner; he demanded respect, to be treated like any other human being, old or young, with a private inward life of his own, with interests and affections to sustain him, with money to his credit—with in short his unimpaired human dignity.

He felt like a man playing out the end game of an important

chess match, from an inferior position, with few pieces for the defence, against an implacable opponent of great skill and greater patience. He felt himself forced back at every move, at every exhausting calculation, to positions which he had to think out in advance; he had always to prepare some further inferior place to go. He must be sure that there was a move open. He had to foresee everything over the short run ahead, think about each thing he did, every step down a short flight of stairs, along the smoothest sidewalk. He had to be careful about stepping off the curb and about stepping onto the sidewalk on the other side of the street, and the green light never stayed on long enough for him to get comfortably across. Every move was planned.

He consulted a doctor regularly, not a man he trusted, a man 25 years his junior. There were no doctors his own age! All the doctors seemed so young.

He had to wear a white shirt this morning because of the funeral. He preferred striped coloured shirts with button-down collars, soft ones that didn't hurt his neck—his shirt size had grown smaller and smaller. He had seen too many old men who wore stiff collars three sizes too big for them, so that they resembled ventriloquists' dummies. He wore soft collars, size thirteen and a half, which was at that a half-size too large, but the softness of the material and the careful way he knotted his tie and held his head erect on his shoulders minimized the scrawniness of his neck and the twistings of its ropy muscles.

He wouldn't select a black tie, didn't in fact own one. He picked out a wide dark wine-coloured knitted silk, held it against the shirt and decided that it was mournful enough. He slid the knot up to his throat, twisting and securing the material. He inserted a pair of expensive silver cufflinks.

Mostly he wore light or dark grey flannel trousers and one of several good jackets and blazers of which he took anxious care. Today he settled on a pair of very dark flannels and a brown Harris tweed which he'd owned for ten years and which was going to outlast him; he sometimes wondered who would get it. Fastening a black armband—which they had sent him —with great distaste, he eased himself into this jacket, admiring the solid tough fabric, and ran his comb once more through his hair. He felt better, now that he was decently dressed, decided that he didn't look so bad after all, made himself some toast and tea, drank a large defiant glass of fruit juice, and sat down to wait for the limousine.

His nephew Alfred had been 62, he thought, or perhaps 63. Mr. Calverly had no children of his own, and had never been close to his brother's children and grandchildren. They were all, he felt, too palpably wondering what he was holding and to whom it was bequeathed. In fact it was willed to them because, while he didn't very much like them or see much of them, he had no patience with those who leave their money and property to charitable institutions and to their pets. He meant his capital to stay in the family, but he never told anybody this. Either they were acute enough to figure it out and didn't need to be told, or they were fools, in which case he saw no necessity of enlightening them.

He was going to the funeral out of a sense of his social duty, not because he felt any perverse pleasure in the fact that he had outlived his nephew. He knew people in their eighties who were amateurs of funerals, connoisseurs of the various undertakers' establishments, who seemed to feel a friendly dilettante interest in such places, a damned outright comfortable nearness to them. He didn't go to funerals from morbidity; but he wouldn't avoid them either if it was a family matter.

At 10.15 his buzzer rang and the man from the undertakers' spoke to him.

"All ready with the car, Mr. Calverly."

He spoke his acknowledgement, went into the bathroom and carefully relieved himself—there might not be another opportunity. That was another concomitant of his situation, the pestering weakness of the bladder. Then he went carefully

82

downstairs and directed the driver to take him to the funeral home.

"The service will be held at the home, won't it?"

"Yes, sir."

"And from there we go directly to the cemetery?"

"Yes, Mr. Calverly."

He didn't participate in the service at the funeral home, feeling physically incapable of remaining on his knees for any length of time. Instead he went into one of the waiting rooms reserved for members of the family and sat, self-contained and dignified, dryly by himself, watching the other people who from time to time put their heads in the door or came and sat down near him. He turned his head from side to side slowly like an ancient tortoise, his hands folded on the knob of his stick.

Once a young man and a young woman whom he knew, his great-nephew and great-niece, came into the room. The girl, who might have been 35, for she had the unformed features of the young, wept silently. The young man smiled helplessly at Mr. Calverly and then, putting his arm around his sister's shoulders, he looked away.

It was all Greek to Mr. Calverly, so remote was he from the ordinary sequence of human affections. There was nobody left for whom he would weep, certainly not his nephew Alfred who had been in many ways, he thought, a foolish opinionated boy, though his designated heir. He remembered suddenly that he would have to alter his will, and wondered which of Alfred's boys this young man was, Pete possibly, or Eddie. He rather liked the look of the young fellow, who seemed to have some genuine care for his sister's feelings. He watched them get up and go out, making a mental note to find out which of his great-nephews this young man might be.

In a little while the drone of voices from the room where Alfred lay began to diminish, paused, then stopped altogether —the service was over. An attendant came in to tell Mr. Calverly that they would now be leaving for the cemetery and that, in accordance with his express request, he would be alone in the third car in the cortege. The attendant offered Mr. Calverly his arm, meaning to conduct him to the waiting car, but he shook him off impatiently, standing in the doorway as the coffin was borne out. He knew none of the pallbearers.

The surprisingly long cortege—he hadn't expected Alfred's departure to be so impressive—took some time to get out of the centre of the city. Mr. Calverly observed the manœuverings of his driver, as the man tried to stay decorously in line, with a certain impatience. He wished that he'd taken the opportunity to visit the Men's Room at the funeral home. A long time spent sitting always put more pressure on his lower abdomen than he could comfortably allow. Soon, however, the procession threaded its way out of the downtown area and began to roll northward along Mount Pleasant Road. He adopted as comfortable a position as he could, leaning against the deep upholstery. The car was very quiet and he was almost tempted to snatch a short nap, but remembered where he was and on what errand, thinking that it wouldn't seem decorous, so he stayed awake and thought about Alfred and about himself.

To that young man and his sister, consoling each other in the waiting room, Alfred Calverly must have seemed the representative of the older generation. It made him chuckle maliciously as he thought of it because he, naturally, considered poor Alfred a callow wet-behind-the-ears youngster whom he'd given his first job; that was 40 years ago when he himself had been a middle-aged veteran of the Stock Exchange.

He realized that for almost everybody Alfred *was* the older generation. And he—he couldn't be placed, for he certainly didn't belong with Alfred. He'd simply outlived all the generations and all the usual human desires and wishes. There was no place further for him to go. He had traded away all his pieces but the last, and there weren't very many more squares on the board to which he might move.

The file of his impressions turned back on itself and blurred, becoming inconsecutive. He felt obscurely that his situation set an insoluble problem in translation. His world didn't exist any more except in history books. Its inhabitants were gone, its manners supplanted. It was as if he were camping out in a totally incomprehensible foreign country where the language was untranslatable because based on absolutely different notions and manners, even the monetary system was different. He still thought of a dollar as a sizeable sum of money out of which one expected change, because it had been so in 1899. It wasn't because he was mean that he hated to leave a paper-money tip. He simply couldn't get used to the new meaning of the old names for money.

The cars stopped on the winding road in Mount Hope Cemetery, and people began to stream along the narrow spaces between the graves to the open excavation in the Calverly plot. Mr. Calverly scrambled out of the limousine, and made his tortoise-like way along behind the throng, taking his time; he had seen all this before.

When he reached the graveside the short burial prayer had been concluded and the cemetery workmen were already lowering the coffin into the ground. People began to chatter amongst themselves and to disperse, some going back, doubtless, to their offices or to lunch, members of the family returning to their altered home. He stood aside and let the crowd flow around him; people jostled him and this made him angry and tired. It had been a long morning. He craned his thin neck and stared down into the grave. Already it was partially filled up. So. There was an end to Alfred. He turned and began to move slowly away to the waiting car, almost the last to go. As he picked his way along, some foolish movement of sorrow and family feeling led him to take his eyes off the uneven footing and stare a last time behind him at the grave. As he did so, he stumbled over a fat lump or tussock of grass and mud and, to his horror and fright, fell full-length on the damp ground.

The lump of grass and mud pressed heavily into the pit of his stomach, nauseating him, and half-supporting him off the grass. He found to his intense shame and discomfort that he was too weak and tired to stand up by himself. He lay there with his arms and legs moving feebly, like a great impaled spider. Once he called out and nobody seemed to hear, and all at once he felt very frightened. He didn't see how to get up.

Then to his relief he felt a hand under his right arm, and another one under his left and against his ribs. A young man's voice said clearly, "You're all right, Uncle Page." He felt himself lifted up, got his feet under him, straightened and looked with gratitude at his saviour. It was the young man whom he'd noticed at the funeral home.

"It is Uncle Page, isn't it?" asked the young man coolly, almost, it seemed to him, with amusement, and he nodded his old head, staring at the young man. And as he stared into the young man's cool eyes, he saw and recognized the stare of the other chess-player. He saw what he'd expected and feared to see for so long, pity in the cool eyes, pity. And behind that, at the back of the remote familiar eyes, contempt.

Worst Thing Ever

Here is a room with light-chocolate coloured walls, windows eight feet by six, chipped and cracked at the sills by long winters. Two rows of beds with cranks underneath dark-brown metal frames; sometimes a high-pitched dribbling babble from behind a tall three-sided white screen. Sun, sun, sun. No sounds of gabby men and women discussing prices, weather, sport, clothing, sex. Instead sound like electronic music, intermittent, without bass, thin and chiming.

"Poor old man, I'll look after you."

"He's too heavy for you, Miss Bevington."

"I was a geriatric nurse before you were born, Sister."

"Aaah-uuuh, eeeigh, aah-aah-aah."

"He's better today, he'll speak soon. You can see the muscle come back, the left eyeball almost under control, skin on the cheek less slack. Wrist twitching. Fingers crawling toward me across the sheet. He knows me, needs me."

". . . never leave here."

"He'll walk out of here beside me, speaking, able to stand up and move, with a cane. I can read the signs."

Next day: "What do you think, Miss Bevington?"

"Oh, good morning Doctor, yes, doing well, this one; you must be proud of him. See him reach out?"

"You know my cases better than I do."

"40 years of it, Doctor. Lonely work."

Rotary floor polisher begins to whir, brush brush, whir on grey plastic tile floor, sound mixing with the old man's whimpers. Now he'll speak for Doctor T. Now, speak now:

"I."

"See?"

"aaiee, aah, uhh. . ."

"Don't wish to disappoint you, Miss Bevington, but that's not exactly speech, is it?"

"Wait a moment."

"I." He hitches up on his elbows, gasps. "I want."

"See?"

"Now he'll see the speech therapist. 89 years old, I wouldn't have believed it."

"I'm taking him home with me."

"You're staying on the case?"

"Family asked me to, nieces, nephews; they've no time for him; they'd be happy to leave him in the ward, but it's knowing you're going home gives you the incentive. He has to have the incentive, you see?"

"Miss Bevington, you deserve all the credit in the world. I'l schedule the speech therapy."

"Now pay attention, Mr. Kekkonen, watch my lips, round. Round, that's it, imitate me. Do you understand me, all right, round? Thaaat's it. Now say: 'Aaaaaaaooooowwwww.' "

"Uuuugh, aauugh."

"Again. Aaaaaooooowwww, round the mouth, draw the lips in around the tongue. That's what we call the point of articulation, you can understand that, I'm sure. Now again."

"Aaaaooooowwww."

"*Very* good."

"Bye-bye, Mr. Kekkonen, bye-bye, Miss Bevington. You listen to what she tells you now, Mr. Kekkonen, be a good boy, plenty of rest. There they go. Heavens, what a will that woman has. You never worked for her, did you, Sister?"

"No, Doctor."

"I'll bet she misses the work. She's taken Kekkonen as a private case, live in, round the clock attention; it'll be like special duty for her. I don't know how long it will last."

"How long would you give him?"

"No telling. The next cerebral heh-heh accident heh-heh, I can never use that phrase without laughing, somehow. Might be six months, might be eighteen months, might be tomorrow. She got him walking and talking anyhow. Quite a triumph for her."

Taxi stops before a comfortable old house, not big, not small, on a quiet street in a middle neighbourhood, might be for the rich or the high-salaried middle-class. When Miss Bevington was born in this house, it was meant for industrious clerks of 50. Houses cost more now. Gordon Bevington knows. "Help with the upkeep," he says.

"I didn't bring him home for that. Say hello to my brother, Pakka."

Quaver from way inside: "Heh heh lo."

"How do you do?"

"Heh lo. I am well."

"Take his arm up the stairs."

"Doesn't seem to want me to. Pulling away."

"How could he pull away from somebody 25 years younger? Come up, Pakka."

Two minutes climbing five stairs, a dangerous ascent for old Kekkonen, whom any fall may finish. Rock and sway in the supporting arm, fog in the eyes, ghastly vertigo, knee joints bending slowly, got to be willed up up enough to plant the foot on the next step. Pure unmixed effort without thought.

"I don't believe he likes me."

"Be quiet, Gordon, he can hear you, can't you Pakka? You hear everything, don't you? Nothing wrong with your hearing, course not, here we are, in we go, this is your room, just like the hospital, nice sunny no stairs to climb you stay in here anything you want we'll bring. Here. Sit here. This is a good chair with the little casters, easy for us to move you. You're going to like it here and we'll take good care of you, yes we will, sit back." Late afternoon now with pleasant shade in the room as the autumn sun moves over the back garden. Gordon Bevington plays a small electric organ in these afternoons, never leaves the house for long, plays softly, trying to amuse the old fellow, find a song he likes; every now and then he'd swear Kekkonen was humming along with the music. "It must be good for him." "Oh, it's the very best thing, there's nothing like soft music in such cases. If you can get him to sing, Gordon, I'll be so grateful."

"Do my best, my dear."

"I know, Gordon, and it must be hard for you, giving up your room. Play 'The Lost Chord' again; he likes that."

"See, see? He *is* singing. That's it, Mr. Kekkonen, you sing, by gosh, do you a world of good. Now I'll play 'There is a Tavern in the Town.' "

"Nothing too rousing, Gordon."

"I'll play the wedding march."

"Oh, Gordon, he'll think you're fishing around, won't you, Pakka?"

"I'm alone."

"You are *not* alone; we're your friends and we'll take care of you forever, you'll see. You'll be safe here, and comfortable and warm."

"I will marry you then."

"Yes. I think that's very wise."

In the spring a lake forms in the back garden when the snow melts, eight inches of chilly black water lapping at the cellar windowpanes. Gordon Bevington stands in his basement bedroom, his head slightly inclined because of the low ceiling, staring through the window at the rising water. If the sun doesn't come soon, the runoff will get into his new apartment, bedroom, kitchenette, bath, sitting-room, and spoil the new furniture, short the TV circuit. My sister married to a 90-year-old Finn. If he could talk, all he could talk would be Finnish or Lettish or some such tongue, all the English he knows is "I want" and "I need" and "He's hurting me." I never did anything to hurt him but you can't lay a hand on him without hurting him, the bones are sticking through paper, not very clean paper either. Can't give him a bath because he might fall in the tub, can't roll him over in bed. What a state! What made her do it? And all because of that I've got to decorate the cellar, floor it, insulate it, furnish and keep clean down here while the house sits up there silent as a terminal ward. Makes me bloody anxious, that does, to think of them up there at night getting ready for him to pass on. Never thought he'd survive the winter, now he's just a big beetle, keeping alive on steam heat and sugar water. Wants to go out for walks! How's he going to go out, tell me that? He can't get out of bed without two people to lift him. It wasn't the money; we have money, plenty. I wonder what rights she has anyway? She's his wife, same as if they'd been married sixty years. If that rain doesn't stop, there'll be water in here tomorrow.

"Gordon? Gordon!"

"What?"

"Can you come quick? Pakka has fallen."

Knew it would come; a matter of time, pure and simple.

Old body inert on the bedroom floor, looking like a crumpled piece of dirty Kleenex, breath of air might blow it away. What's he broken? Hip, most likely. "Should we call the doctor?"

Mrs. Kekkonen wrings her hands. "I just don't know what he's done to himself. I can't locate a fracture but at his age you can't be sure. I only left the room for a minute and he must have tried to follow me, or get to the bathroom."

"He's never tried that, since I've known him."

"Don't leave him on the floor, Gordon. Oh, the poor thing, oh."

"Breathing all right."

"I know he's breathing; do you think I can't tell when a patient's breathing, the life I've led? The trouble is, I don't know whether he's comatose. Perhaps we'd better lift him."

They hoist the old body onto the bed, smooth the sheets, straighten out the threadlike legs. A moth, that's what he's like, broken moth, chest lifting almost invisibly, quiet bubbling of breath and a silver trickle of spittle down the grey chin. As Gordon stares at the still face, one eye rolls weirdly open and fixes him. No sound, no bleeding, what's to be done?

"Nothing to do but wait."

"Wait?"

"He can't survive, can he?"

"Get me a chair."

She sits at the bedside, leans forward and watches. Except for sleeping, occasional food, and attending to her bodily functions, she sits there for six months as spring turns to summer and then to fall. Sitting waiting, no change, a long dying almost indistinguishable from a 90-year life. The death is born in the old man's fall; it's baby death when they lift him from the floor, death like the infancy of God, harmless, swaddled, innocent, attractive. Baby Death.

It's a long time growing, lies in its crib learning to move its little arms, cooing and gurgling. It tries to stand up but can't manage its legs, such a cute baby, living in the universe of the ancient man's body, solitary inhabitant. . . takes a long time to grow a single death. In summer it stands and moves around: teenage death, awkward and unsure, sometimes repellent, often pitiable, weak, blank, unaware of its strength.

Young manhood and the show of independence. I can finish you like that. Like that! Snap of the fingers death. See? Mrs. Kekkonen tries to carry the body to the sunporch and tears something in her abdomen, bringing the doctor to the house. "Big as a baseball, how'd you do that?" "I tried to carry him; he's light." "He's light but he weighs 80 pounds all the same, that's too much for you, that's almost your own weight." "I weigh 90 pounds." "Don't go picking up your own weight then; you're an elderly woman."

I AM NOT NOT NOT.

"Whatever you are, you've got a very troublesome hernia, so don't go lifting anything again. Afterward we'll have that fixed; it's a simple operation. Eat. Be well."

"Afterward."

"When he's dead."

"Doctor, tell me, technically, where does death begin and end? Is it possible for it to go on so long?"

"We're all dying. You know that."

"Then the word has no scientific meaning. It's a name for part of the biological cycle."

"If it helps you to think of it that way, yes."

"I don't need any help."

"You're very fortunate."

Death the big strong man grows older as the fall comes on, and weaker, in symbiosis with his dwelling. They live on each other and become attenuated in a race to the finish line which ends in a tie, though the line isn't a line but a vague area of obscure limits. Brain function flattens out and can't be recorded in meaningful patterns. Respiration and circulation less and less adequate; remote tissues are threatened, then damaged. No line is crossed. No-one can tell when dying ceases to exist, but finally in the third week of November there is agreement that whatever this thing is, it isn't a human body. One biochemical system succeeds another; there is no more dying going on.

Then Mrs. Kekkonen gets out of her chair and goes to the breakfast room for cereal and cream, hurting every step of the way, lump in her abdomen swelling. One thing about being a nurse, they give you royal treatment in the hospital. She calls her old subordinates and they set the visit up, best of everything, round the clock attention and quick-recovery procedures.

"I'll be in a week, Gordon, I know you'll manage."

"You should have gone before."

"Couldn't go then, with Pakka terminal."

"You call that terminal? Some terminal, bloody big terminal that was, to take so long."

"Phone me if you need anything. I don't think the funeral will be a problem."

"He's gone and left the house full of it. How will we get it out? I have to live here too, you know. I didn't expect this."

"The cab is at the door. Would you bring my overnight case?"

"Overnight case, overnight case. Take care of yourself."

"You can call me at any time. There's no pain involved."

"Pain is always involved and I never knew that before. Imagine!"

Mrs. Kekkonen is in the hospital. I'm sorry, Mrs. Kekkonen is in the hospital, no, I'm sorry, she's not here, she's in the hospital.

"What, at a time like that? Doesn't seem right somehow, seems like she ought to be at the funeral, a woman's place is at her husband's side at a time like this, seems to me. You'd kind of expect that, wouldn't you, at least I would. I mean, she was his legal wife and that's what counts. I don't suppose they could ever have had uh, marital uh relations, not at his age."

"You'd be surprised."

"No I wouldn't. I hope he left a will."

"She's his wife legally, could complicate things."

"It will complicate things."

"It has complicated things."

"Have you ever heard of a custom they have in India, where the widow gets buried alongside of the husband? Must make things simpler."

"What did he want to go and get married for?"

"Why would she marry him?"

"You may well ask."

Mrs. Kekkonen is in the hospital.

Gordon Bevington is on the porch roaring at his neighbour, a timid man. "Worst thing ever happened to me, this last year has been, you wouldn't believe what I've been through. My sister isn't strong; you've seen her up and down the street. A wonderful woman to shop. Of course I never ate with them after she brought him home. I go up to the corner and I buy these cans of meatballs and gravy, says on the label serves four, and it serves one, me, a good dinner for one. I do my own cooking; it's not as if I were dependent. You haven't seen my self-contained living quarters, kitchen with self-scrubbing Formica counter bound in light metal stripping, plastic tile flooring up over the drain, designed by Specialty Home Improvements for maximum convenience and utilization of potential living space. It's a little jewel: solid comfort. I get in there nights with my colour TV with automatic tuning control and safe-switching rheostat and I don't even get out of bed. She never went to bed at all for seven months, did you know. You've seen her shop. She told me once you helped her carry in a carton of tomato juice. She's like that, watches the specials, goes and buys 24 cans of juice that she won't use in a year. Brings it home by herself. I was glad you helped her. She shouldn't lift heavy weights like that. It was lifting that put her in the hospital. She'd pick him up and carry him from the bedroom to the sunroom. I did my best, I tried to help. He wouldn't let me come near him, used to make an awful noise, not a loud noise but one that stuck in your head, a sound like steam coming through a pinhole. Didn't like me, I don't know why. I did the best I could but he wouldn't let me touch him, so she'd pick him up and carry him and the result is she's in the hospital. If she hadn't picked him up once in a while, he'd have been in his bed the whole time. Couldn't get to the toilet naturally, that would be expecting too much, poor old thing. We had to look after him that way. . . know what I mean. There was nothing. Just water. Well sir, and then there was his family around. Bonnie flew in from Vancouver and came to the house yesterday. Who's Bonnie? I never heard of any Bonnie, there she is on the porch. 'I'm Bonnie from Vancouver.' She's in the hall. 'Oh the Benares brass cigarette box. Uncle Pakka told me that was mine. He wanted me to have it. I'll just take that along, if you don't mind.' Puts it in her shopping bag. 'Where are the commemorative medals of Finnish independence?' 'What?' 'Uncle Pakka was in the National Assembly.' 'Medals like big round copper disks the size of almost a saucer?' 'That's them.' 'Well Bonnie, I'm sorry to say somebody came and took those away yesterday. I wondered what they were; couldn't read the writing naturally.' 'They were very valuable. I hope you have a correct inventory.' 'What of?' 'Uncle Pakka's belongings.' 'I don't know about that but my understanding is a husband and wife share what they have.' 'That will all have to be cleared up.' "

"It was an awful thing, my sister away, all the arrangements to be made. She keeps asking about the bills. I tell her not to worry about the bills; the lawyers can take care of them. She worries anyway. Couldn't do anything else, the way she is. I don't understand her at all. Then that family, don't understand them either, worst thing ever happened to me, I tell you."

The Pitcher

"Il n'y a pas de mystère dans la création humaine. La volonté fait ce miracle. Mais du moins, il n'est pas de vraie création sans secret."

—Camus, *La Création absurde*

There was once a tired businessman like you or me or Sherwood Anderson, a bachelor verging on middle age, fat, flabby and 37, who suddenly received word one sunny showery blue and white April afternoon that an elderly relative had died in Australia, bequeathing him an immense legacy.

Hod Gantenbein, for that was his name, had read somewhere and remembered that the truly vicious man, stepping on an ant, hopes it hurts. The observation had so impressed him that he would tread on no living thing on the sidewalk; when he saw small green caterpillars struggling on the cement he lifted them tenderly and put them in the grass, where they might survive. He made an exception of the common *musca domestica*, that germ-carrier and breeder of disease, but even these he merely shooed out of his house with a rolled-up newspaper, rather than do them bodily harm.

When he heard of his aunt's death he was at first reluctant to receive his inheritance, on the grounds that the money was infected by the dear old lady's pain. Only a series of cablegrams between Hartford and Melbourne, which established that his Aunt Grace had died peacefully in her sleep, full of years and in the certitude of a glorious resurrection, had persuaded him to accept his property. As a general rule he was opposed to inheritance, holding that death is painful, and that it is the condition of testament. He would scorn, he declared, he would scorn to profit by another's agony.

In the middle of May the money arrived in America in the form of a draft on The Corn and Fleece Bank and Trust of Victoria and New South Wales in the amount of $200,000, a sum which Gantenbein calculated would just serve his burgeoning purposes, permitting him the five free years necessary for the project he had in mind, an imagining of which he had long despaired, but which he was now enabled to realize. And though he was a responsible citizen, holding a responsible post as the director and programmer of a fleet of punch-card machines in the Hartford home offices of Monolithic Life, he gave up his job at once, not like a foolish sweepstakes winner, intoxicated by good fortune and bereft of good judgment, but like one who sees looming before him his very last chance to enact his dearest fantasy.

So transparent were his motives that his employers indulged him. They refused to accept his resignation and told him instead that he might have as much leave as he liked, to get it out of his system, but they weren't going to let him quit, no sir, he was too valuable a man to lose.

"It will take five years," he said, trying to be fair, "I'm allowing myself five years, and if it doesn't work out, I'll come back at the end of that time. I wish you'd let me quit."

"No!"

"I can't quit? Not at all?"

"Never! Take all the time you want."

There was something about this insistence that inwardly bothered him; but he thought it wise not to think about it too much. What must he do, he wondered, to persuade them to release him? Apparently sudden riches were not enough; sickness wouldn't do it, for the company had paid all the expenses of employees who had been invalid for decades. Old age and death, he decided, would get a man out of Monolithic, and per-

haps abandoned vice, but about the last he was not certain—
they would call it sickness.

His money safely on deposit, he left town and motored to
a health farm in upstate New York, 40 miles southwest of
Plattsburgh. This curious establishment was the property of
the ex-lightweight champion Gummy Broomstein, an almost
legendary figure of the ring, who could stand on a handkerchief
and let you swing at him all day without getting hit. That is,
he could have done it 40 years ago; now when he tried it tired
businessmen punched the hell out of him.

Gummy couldn't stop trying this trick though. He would
spread the handkerchief carefully on the grass, stand on it, and
say thickly: "Try and hit me, go ahead, try and hit me," bob-
bing and weaving all the time and keeping his hands at his
sides. Then somebody would paste him one on the side of the
head, and he would step off the handkerchief, looking down
at it reproachfully.

"Caught me cold," he would mumble, "a sneak punch."

Gummy was glad to welcome Hod Gantenbein, a new and
wealthy client who had announced by letter his intention of
staying at the farm for as long as a year, if it were necessary,
and really getting into shape, *really*.

"Can a man of 37 *really* get into shape?" said Hod to Gummy, when they met at the gate.

"Fitzsimmons held the title when he was 40," said Gummy,
"and look at Archie Moore. Look at Walcott."

"Marciano stopped Walcott in a minute 40 seconds."

"Yeah, but the things is you had a man of 40 in there with
the champion, I mean, that's unusual."

"I don't want to box, though," said Hod, reflectively.

"Why do you want to get in shape?"

"I intend to become a pitcher," said Hod, whose imagination
had been nurtured on *Lefty Locke of the Blue Stockings* and
other Saalfeld publications of the early 1900s. He thought
perpetually of the horsehide, the rubber, the initial and key-

99

stone sacks, the hot corner, the outer gardens, and his imaginative life seemed to have been checked somewhere about the end of the Christy Mathewson era.

"Well, Jeeze," said Gummy, "a pitcher uses all the wrong muscles."

"Wrong for boxing, you mean, but I want to pitch."

"How long have you got?"

"I intend to spend a year on this phase."

"In a year I can get you ready to go fifteen rounds."

"But can you get me ready to go nine innings?"

"Yes, I can do that too. But you'll be using *all* the wrong muscles."

"Never mind," said Hod, "it's what I want to do."

"Then I'll see you at 6.30 tomorrow," said Gummy as he showed him to his room, "and remember, from now on no alcohol and no tobacco, and a balanced diet which I'll draft when I've had a look at you."

Tired from the variety of new sounds and sensations, Hod went to bed early, setting his alarm for six. He had been accustomed to rise at eight, and was looking forward to seeing a sunrise or two, feeling obscurely that the experience would ennoble him, make him a better man. It never did, of course, but then he was pretty good to start with.

Next morning after a breakfast of eggs, bacon, buttered toast and plenty of strong tea, Gummy led Hod to the gymnasium, where he meant to look him over.

"I warn you," said Hod, "I'm as far out of condition as possible. I've been sitting down for the last twenty years." He put on the shorts and t-shirt and track shoes that Gummy handed him, and fidgeted embarrassedly while the trainer assessed him.

"Boy!" said Gummy. He walked around and around Hod. "Boy!"

"Awful, isn't it?"

"You weigh around 195, right?"

"Dead on."

"You'll lose 40, 50, pounds of that in the next two months. You're just carrying around a load of fat, no wonder all you guys have heart attacks. Look at you, look at that stomach!" He prodded Hod disgustedly. "After we get you down around 150 you'll start to get some muscle tone, and then you'll gain. But it'll be muscle, not fat. You're around six feet tall, so you should weigh, with your bones, around 178. We're going to take it off your stomach and your ass and put it on your shoulders and chest, *and* we're going to build up your legs. If you're going to be a pitcher you've got to have the legs, and yours are like a girl's. If you did twenty knee bends, you'd have a case of jag legs."

"How do we start?"

"We run. That is, you run." He pointed. "Eleven times around the track is a mile. Get up there and go a mile. Sprint the last two laps and I'll time you."

When Hod had jogged nine laps, he couldn't sprint, so he walked the last two, and Gummy timed him in eleven minutes, 42 and seven-tenths seconds. His legs felt like spaghetti stalks and he collapsed gasping on a bench. He could taste every cigarette he'd ever smoked.

"The record for the mile is 3:54," said Gummy coldly, "you've got a long way to go."

"What do we do now?" demanded Hod, tottering to his feet.

"We run some more. That is, you do."

So for weeks he ran and ran and ran. He ran against a stopwatch in the gym. He did wind sprints for hours on the back lot, a hundred feet and stop, hours and hours. He did roadwork in the country with Gummy pacing him on a bicycle, uphill and down, he ran and ran and ran, and his wind and vision improved and his head cleared; he began to taste his food, he forgot about cigarettes, and his time for the mile came down. When he wasn't running he was doing pushups and situps and knee bends and chinning himself and throwing the medicine ball and playing squash and following a high protein diet and he began to notice some changes.

Like what? Well he didn't feel like himself any more. A man goes along for the first half of his life feeling the way most of us do, you and me and Sherwood, and he comes to believe that being human logically implies the constant faint headache, the slightly out of focus eyes, the shitty taste in the mouth, the sour stomach and the unending dosages of antacids, dandruff removers, deodorants, laxatives, breath sweeteners, and all this while he silently hates his body and mistreats it, this albatross around his oh so spiritual neck, for inflicting life on him, sleeps poorly, eats like a fool, and gives himself no chance.

Hod meant to give himself this latest of chances, and it made all the difference. Whereas he used to have troubling dreams, waking every morning with an erection and wounded sexual feelings, now he slept like the dead and was no longer tormented by desire and guilt, and he understood why Gummy and Charley and Whitey and most of the other old trainers bar wives from fight camps. It isn't done out of latent homosexuality, as he'd always naïvely supposed; it's simply that the question of women ceases to come up. There is a time for everything. Full genitality (that genial *summum bonum* of the 1960s) is not the sole end and purpose of human life. Insert the phrase in one of the old songs and it becomes absurd:

> Sweet personality,
> Full genitality,
> That's Peggy O'Neill.

He got his time for the mile down around five minutes, and then into the fours. His heart stopped pounding and his lungs stopped burning when he went a fast mile. He would never do it in 3:54, and wouldn't have to; he didn't have the reflexes and the lung capacity of a great miler, but he pushed closer every day to the absolute outside limit that his particular body, legs just this length, rib cage this size, might at last achieve.

Then Gummy put him on a pattern of calisthenics to develop his muscle tone, working on each part of the body in turn, the shoulders and arms, the neck, abdomen, legs, joints, his weight began to move up again and finally hovered around 175 until it was evident that he was a natural light-heavyweight and would never weigh more than 178 as long as he stayed in shape. They began to spar a couple of rounds at a time and Hod at once discovered that he might be physically perfect, medically, and still be unable to box more than a single three-minute round at a time.

"When you can go fifteen fast rounds, shadow-box for an hour, work on the bags for another two hours, run ten miles, and finish with 50 lengths in the pool," said Gummy, "you can start throwing a ball because you'll be ready."

"And when I'm learning to pitch I'll have to do all these things besides?"

"Sure. For an athlete you're an old man. I doubt we can bring your reflexes up to the point where you can play pro ball."

"Yes we can," said Hod stoutly, for he was very determined.

"The only edge you'll have on the kids will be condition. You'll outrun them and outwork them. But they'll have skills that you don't have."

"I'll get the skills," said Hod, "I'll spend the next year on that."

In the spring, when he had completed phase one of his design, he started combing *The Sporting News* for the names of out-of-work catchers. He compiled a list of six names, men who had been released in spring training. Then he sent them individual letters offering a year's employment at their last major-league salary and he received two replies, one from Joe Fritz, a cagey ten-year veteran of the majors whose throwing arm had finally gone, and the other from Luther Hollings, a promising rookie cut by the Gold Sox who had gone home in disgust.

Hod thought it would be better to work with an experienced major-leaguer, so he sent young Hollings a polite letter and a cheque for his trouble; but to Joe Fritz he sent an urgent wire, and a cheque for expenses and one month's salary. Three days later the veteran receiver appeared at the farm, a stumpy-legged man with a gnarled black face and fingers like bananas. Together Gummy and Hod explained the project, and Joe could scarcely believe his ears.

"You want to make a ballplayer out of this fellow? Has he ever played?"

"I played in high school," said Hod, "and it's unbelievable what you can do, if you work hard enough."

"He's in terrific shape," said Gummy proudly.

"I can see that," said Joe, "the way he can run. But you have to know the game. Can he throw at all?"

"My arm has never been used," said Hod, "literally. There ought to be a lot of spring in it."

"We'll see," said Joe, "and you say you've got a year to work?"

"I plan to report to some training camp next spring."

"And you're 38?"

"Warren Spahn is 40."

"But he's one of the five greatest pitchers in history."

"If he can pitch in the majors at 40," pursued Hod inexorably, "so can I."

Joe Fritz was astonished at Hod's attitude and determination but didn't believe the thing could be done. "I can maybe teach you enough to hang on in Class D for a month or two," he decided, "but you'll have to be satisfied with that."

"We'll see," said Hod, and he led the old catcher to an improvised diamond on the back lot, where he began to throw. His arm felt strong and good.

"Is that the hardest you can throw?" asked Joe cynically.

"It is today," said Hod, "but it won't be next year. I've got to teach myself to get my body into the pitch. I weigh 178 and I ought to be able to get enough leverage to throw fast."

"Right now you throw like José Morales," said Joe glumly, "still, it's your money. Tell you what, if you get so you can do anything at all, we'll play some semi-pro ball the end of the summer." They began to work in earnest. First Joe had his pupil throw and throw without putting anything on the ball, to develop a smooth motion and get the necessary leverage. Gummy took movies of Hod, and the three men studied them after supper until bedtime. The ball began to buzz over the plate.

"Say," said the catcher one morning after they'd been working together for two months, "say, that ball took off, it had some hop on it." He began to show real interest in the project for the first time. "Right now you're sneaky fast, not real fast but faster than you look. But you'll have to be really fast, because we haven't time to give you another pitch."

"Yes we have," said Hod, "I want a change of pace and a curve. Next year I'll pick up a slider, but I want the three basic pitches straight off, so I'll have a chance to stick."

"Come on, then," said Joe, "hum that seed in there. Sneaky fast won't get you anywhere." They threw and threw. They hammered together wooden frames of differing dimensions and erected these in front of the plate for Hod to throw at.

"This here is the strike zone that Minnie Minoso gives you," said Joe, planting one of these frames in the ground, "let's see how you'd pitch him." In August Hod was working on control, pitching to the inch and a half of space that borders the strike zone, resolved that like his heroes Matthewson and Spahn he would never throw one down the pipe, an act he considered as immoral as stepping on a bug.

"You can control the straight pitch," said Joe, one day late in August, "and you've got a lot on it, the fast ball takes off. Maybe we better concentrate on that for the rest of the year."

"I'll never make the majors with one pitch."

105

"I dunno, you might fool them all for one swing around the league. You might win a few at the end of a season." They were thinking about the same thing: spring him on the league at the end of a hot pennant race.

"Like Duren did, that one year," said Hod.

"Yeah, or Joe Page or Wilcy Moore, you're good for one season maybe. We better throw you at somebody in semi-pro." Using his extensive contacts, the old catcher arranged an appearance for them as a battery with a club playing out of Oneonta, N.Y. They drove over one Friday in early September, and next afternoon Hod shut out the opposition on two hits, striking out nineteen, throwing nothing but fast balls.

"Could he do that again?" asked the manager of the Oneonta team.

"Maybe once more with that club," said Joe dourly, "but he doesn't know how to mix them up, he needs another pitch." From September through Christmas the two men, now equally dedicated to the grand purpose, worked ten hours a day on a change of pace thrown with the same motion as the fast ball, and when they had it perfected they began to develop a rudimentary curve. Toward the end of the second phase of the project Hod could throw three pitches with the identical sweeping three-quarters arm motion. He had a naturally smooth beautiful delivery, which is something not all pitchers have and which can't be acquired artificially.

"Lordy, Lordy," said Joe Fritz, one afternoon in February, "I wish we had another year to teach you a motion to first, and when to come in with the first pitch."

"No time," said Hod succinctly, "I've got to get into pro ball this season. You've got to get me a job."

Joe wrote letters to all his friends who were managing in the minors. Most of them showed no interest but at length Yancey Hooker, the old flychaser, now managing the Lancaster Groundhogs, agreed to give Hod a look-see, provided that he paid his own training camp expenses. Hod and Joe drove down to Lancaster, reported in at the front office, and then proceeded to the camp, at Hudson, Fla.

"Yancey Hooker, you crooked old buzzard," said Joe excitedly when he spied the manager, "I haven't seen you since we played together at Terre Haute in the Three I League, twenty years ago."

"Yeah, never mind that," said Hooker sourly, "what about this boy Gantenbein, has he got anything?"

"Wait'll you see him," said Joe.

Hod pitched batting practice the first week of the camp, during which Manager Hooker began to realize that this odd poised determined 39-year-old rookie might indeed have something. At the beginning of the second week he started Hod in an intra-squad game.

Out there on the hill, Hod was nervous as he took his warm-up pitches, wondering whether to come in there with the first pitch. His catcher called for the fast ball low on the outside corner, and Hod remembered that nobody these days ever, ever, delivers the ball high. He delivered the ball where it was called for and the batter drove a sharp liner back through the box. Instinctively Hod stuck up his glove to protect himself and the ball lodged in the pocket, stinging his palm, for the first out. He went three innings and didn't allow a hit, striking out five. In the third inning he came off the mound to his right and fielded a bunt perfectly, easily beating the runner with his throw, and after his stint was over he overheard Manager Hooker talking excitedly to the lone Lancaster reporter who was travelling with the Groundhogs.

"This fellow Gantenbein is going to help the club," said the grizzled pilot with enthusiasm, "he fields his position like a cat out there, just like a cat. Reminds me of Harry Brecheen."

"Or Bobby Shantz," said the reporter knowledgeably.

"No," said Hooker, "Shantz is just a little guy."

"Where did Gantenbein pitch last year?" asked the reporter skeptically.

"Ganty?" said Hooker vaguely, "he struck out everybody he faced in semi-pro ball last year, up in New York somewhere." This was partly true, as we know.

"Ganty," for the nickname was to cling, had no book on the hitters, but equally they had none on him. By the middle of July at the All Star break, six major-league scouts were following the club. Hod had won seventeen and lost none, and his ERA was the lowest in baseball, a startling 0.83. His contract belonged to the Lancaster club of course, and after spirited bidding for his services they sold him to the New York Toads organization. The Toads shipped him immediately to their Denver farm club where he won six in a row through August, giving him a record of 23 wins and no losses on the season. On the last day before he would be ineligible for a Series appearance the Toads called him up to the parent club to help out in the stretch drive; they were nursing a two-and-a-half game lead and faced a series with the second-place Detroit Bombs with their pitching in disarray. When Hod reported in the dressing-room, the Toads' famous old skipper Grumpy Hazebrouck took him into his office alone, to have a look at him.

"So you're 'Ganty,' my goodness," said Grumpy, looking at the pitcher's face, deeply tanned and wrinkled from his summer in the sun, "you mean to tell me you're a rookie? How old are you anyway?"

"39."

"That's too old."

"Warren Spahn is 41," said Hod automatically, for he'd been repeating it to himself all year.

"By criminy," said Grumpy, "I may have to use you this weekend and I hope you can pitch as good as you talk."

"I can," said Hod, and the manager made a gesture of dismissal.

Little now remains to be told: of how Hod saved four games in a row in relief, brushing the hitters back and throwing them offstride with a judicious mixture of his four pitches—he'd picked up a slider during his summer in the minors; how in the waning days of the season he started and went the route for the win three times, finishing the season with a record of five and nothing and an ERA of 1.06; how in the Series he came on in the first game with the bases loaded and shut out the opposition for six innings, how in the fourth game he saved the win for plucky little Ernest Beecham, and how he started and won in eleven innings in the seventh game, covering himself with glory, and how, astonishingly, his Toad teammates voted him a full share in the Series money, and how at last, ten days after the season was over, on his fortieth birthday, he announced his retirement from baseball.

At the loss of "Ganty" the world of sport was thunderstruck. At a hastily-assembled press conference at the Plaza, Hod stood composedly with Gummy and Joe on either side of him, while reporters from 500 dailies besieged him with questions.

"We know all about you, Ganty," chorused the scribes, "how you suddenly quit your job three years ago to take up the diamond sport. Everybody in Hartford, and in the whole country, is talking about what you've done. It's a great triumph of human aspiration. But what are you going to do now?"

"Well," said Hod slowly, "I've got a lot of money and over two years left. I thought it would take five, and it only took half the time. I was out two and a half years in my reckoning." He seemed annoyed at his error.

"Yes, but what will you do?"

"I don't know," he said, "I may do some big-game hunting."

"And can you tell us as an inspiration to American youth what made you attempt this thing?"

"Of course," said Hod simply, politely, and it was to be his last public word, "I just wanted to see if it could be done."

The Hole

Laidlaw sat at the counter on a wobbly stool in Sam and Kitty's diner, looking at the hole in a doughnut, wondering if it was correct to speak of the hole as if it really existed. How could he be looking at a hole? There was nothing to see. He was of the opinion, without having thought the matter through with rigour, that the doughnut was actually comprised of the solid brown mass of cooked batter forming the ringlike object he held in his hand, which undeniably circled a space. Surely you couldn't claim that this space was in the batter, exactly... could you?

The doughnut did not include the space; the doughnut was what you could eat. When you had eaten the fried dough you hadn't consumed a hole.

He meditated upon crullers, straight uncircular twists of material, and upon doughnuts with no holes, more like cakes than anything else, blobs, droppings, twists.

Kitty the waitress, an old friend, spoke to him. "Something the matter with that?"

Laidlaw said, "I'm thinking about it."

This speech made the other customers in the diner laugh very hard. "What's to think?" said Berger from the hardware store. "Too big of a hole for such a little doughnut?" asked a burly truckdriver, one of the regulars.

"Shhh," warned Kitty, who had a reverence for Laidlaw because he was a professor, "leave him be." Silence fell; there were a few further half-hearted attempts at mirth and eating, but in a little while all the other customers filed out one after another, leaving Laidlaw almost alone with Kitty, in silent reflection.

When the doughnut machine extrudes the batter, he thought, just as it is being squeezed out of the tip of the batter-squeezer, no hole exists. There is no hole already in being, waiting for the mix to be wrapped around it. He remembered some comedians' proposals for the sale of different kinds of stoppers, like Henry Morgan's imaginary product, Morgan's Minty Middles, designed to go with Life Savers. If you inserted a Minty Middle in a Life Saver you were not really filling a hole, you were bringing together two pieces of matter which had no existential connection. They were mutually alienated.

If you changed a flat tire, you didn't consider the hub as being inside the new wheel, exactly. That seemed to be because the surface of neither the wheel nor the hub was broken. But suppose you put a Minty Middle into a Life Saver, then sucked the two candies till they ran together, couldn't you then say that the one candy had gotten inside the other?

Laidlaw stuck his forefinger through the hole in his doughnut in a gesture of distinct erotic substance; the waitress snickered.

He ate the doughnut. "Give me a fresh one," he mumbled with his mouth full. Kitty brought another, and fresh coffee, and looked hard into his eyes, which were glazed somewhat alarmingly.

He was now thinking about surfaces, and the impenetrability of matter, and wondering finally, as he had many times before, whether any one thing could ever be said really to get inside anything else, whether any surface was ever penetrated. For if two things grew together, or were so united as not to be distinguishable in space, they seemed to be a single thing.

Married people were only metaphorically said to be sexually united. Sexual congress consisted merely in the insertion of one body in a vacant space, with surfaces which defined it all around, to be sure, but quite impenetrable surfaces. It was characteristic of Laidlaw in all innocence to consider sexuality strictly within the confines of the married state. His cosmological point, however, was sound.

Inside and outside: purely relative. He imagined a cube of polished granite, one foot by one foot by one foot. Suppose you wanted to get inside that stone. You might take a sledgehammer and break it apart. Then all you would have would be several irregularly shaped smaller pieces of granite, and you would not be inside any of them. You might then reduce these pieces to a fine crystalline powder. And then suppose you picked out a single speck of the powder and magnified it under a powerful microscope—it would still exist, solid and complete, an impenetrable thing.

Laidlaw now began to be aware of a phenomenon which had always disturbed his thinking: he felt strongly tempted to fall asleep. There was something powerfully soporific about this kind of speculation: perhaps it was dangerous, and this was nature's warning.

He shook his head vigorously, and fought off the urge to sleep or self-hypnosis. From the kitchen, the waitress and her husband, the short-order cook, watched him anxiously.

"I wish he wouldn't do that here," said Sam, the cook, in some distress of mind. Once or twice before Laidlaw had meditated so deeply in the diner that he had put himself into a state of catalepsy, and had had to be carried off, stiff as a board, in a condition which terrified Kitty and Sam. They were afraid they might have poisoned him.

"He's falling into another trance," said Kitty.

But this was not so. Under his appearance of immobility and near-trance, Laidlaw had never been so active; his mind raced backward, round and round circling avenues of reasoning, trying to think of some mode of being in which one thing was inside another thing and yet distinct from it. He briefly considered the condition of the child in the womb, then rejected it as unacceptable. He began to guess that individual bits

112

of matter were incommunicable; but if that were so, how did they associate themselves together so as to form what we call things?

Whenever he reached this stage in a sequence of reasoning long familiar to him, Laidlaw felt a dreadful shudder of revulsion from his own body, which at these moments he considered a loose and arbitrary, accidental, coming together of bits of stuff that had no reason to coalesce. His body was a ghastly irrational accident. The notion made him want to vomit, and he always used the same stratagem to repress nausea.

> For in your beauty's orient deep
> These flowers, as in their causes, sleep.

He would recite these lines from Carew's beautiful poem over and over to himself, like an incantation or prayer, until the notion of a thing's existing in its cause seized his imagination and banished his nausea.

Now he began to think of containment in other than merely physical terms. Instead of seeing physical proximity, like that of the water against the sides of a well, as a terrifying puzzle (how could any bit of water be next to any other bit, as all water seemed to be sliding around all the time), his mind resigned matter to its own peculiar conditions of inscrutability and ascended to the consideration of immaterial things. Matter was likely better left unthought; he could make nothing of it. He smiled.

"Now he's going to be all right," said the waitress. "He won't pass out on us this time." She came out of the kitchen and rattled saucers on the masonite counter. "Professor," she said softly, then louder, "Professor Laidlaw."

Coming to with a jump he mumbled,

> Ask me no more where Jove bestows,
> When June is past, the fading rose.

"Fading?" said Kitty. "Fading? Sex! That's all you ever think about." She gave a discreet cough.

"More coffee. I need to stay awake."

"It's early afternoon."

"Never mind that. I feel sleepy."

"That is what we all feel very much concerned about," said Kitty.

The professor said, "Don't be frightened. There's no danger."

"Are you certain?"

"Perfectly. A harmless matter of metaphysical speculation."

For some reason this alarmed Kitty a lot. She wished he would do his metaphysical speculations somewhere else, but hesitated to speak out. She watched with fascination and perplexity as his face cleared, his eyes rounded, and he sank into meditation.

"This isn't the place," she said irritably, but he couldn't hear. He was far off down a new chain of thought. "In their causes. *In* their causes." In what way could a flower be said to be in its cause? Bits of traditional philosophical language rose up in memory. Causality, necessary and sufficient, formal, material, efficient and final. Suppose a musician had composed a whole overture in his head, without ever having written it down, could you then say that this was a genuine case of something's being inside something else? Or was it inaccurate to say that the piece of music existed before it was written down in an observable public state on music manuscript paper? Did the act of publication then create the work? It seemed ridiculous to maintain that an overture, unperformable because not in score, neverthless existed somehow or other. And yet it did, because the composer could hear it. This had notoriously been the case with W.A. Mozart.

How about poems, or the ideas for paintings?

"*In* their causes."

Naturally this kind of thinking led Laidlaw, trained as a philosopher for many years, to the notion of the Deity, a notion which had always at once fascinated and repelled him. His idea of Deity was wholly impersonal, an Aristotelian Unmoved Mover, the pattern of all things, perhaps the physical source of motion and biological change, but not personal—simply the stopgap by which philosophers avoided an unthinkable infinite regress, when they speculated about the edge of the universe.

"In their *causes*?"

Uncaused causes, unmoved movers, same thing. Obviously you couldn't think of more than one uncaused cause, or unmoved mover. Why not? Why couldn't you have parallel series of infinite regression, without contact between the series? That would be absurd, wouldn't it? For it would presuppose two, perhaps more than two, infinite things, which appeared to be contradictory; there could not be two or more infinite things. If they were really multiple, they would be limited by one another.

His chest heaved; he screwed his eyes tightly shut in an effort to concentrate. He didn't want to be interrupted.

Sam went to the door and hung a sign in the window. It said CLOSED. Over his shoulder he asked Kitty, "Has anybody ever ruptured themselves just thinking?"

With his eyes shut tight like that, and his chest inflated, the Waynflete Professor of Mental and Moral Philosophy at the provincial university resembled a bullfrog. He would have been pleased by this resemblance, never liking to consider himself removed from the other elements of creation. Blown up so, hardly breathing, he looked like a balloon or a big puffball which might suddenly float up into the air and away out the window. Outside it was early June, about 2.30 in the afternoon of a hazy, mildly sunny day. Students from the university came and went, their faces twisted in the agony of the examination season.

Professor Laidlaw was supposed to be in his office, grading exam papers; some students, observing that he philosophized most intensely at this time of year, claimed that metaphysics was a form of escape for him.

"His intense apprehension of the real is a crutch,"they would say, and the brighter students would go on to propose some paradox about illusion being socially more real than an intuitive perception of a higher truth. To do him justice, Professor Laidlaw would not have entertained such a paradox for an instant if he had been around to hear it.

As things were, sitting in Sam and Kitty's place, the stink of rancid deep-fry in his nose, the faint creaking of the stool under him suggesting that he might fall off it at any moment, he had passed beyond the level of easy paradox into a region of severe and taxing concentration, a kind of effort not many people are called upon to make. Real thought is rare, and feels funny; it's hard on you, and you can't keep it up too long.

Why could there be no more than one infinite entity? Obviously because there couldn't be anything outside of it. If some being were infinite, it would be infinite through time and space, or rather it would extend beyond time and space and enclose them; but it would not enclose them as finite things are enclosed in space. The way an infinite being surrounded things would be different from the way space defined cubes of granite, or human beings or bullfrogs. An infinite being would be omnipresent; therefore it would extend itself necessarily through all other things, and nothing would be separate from it.

"In God we live and move and have our being."

Was it unthinkable that there might be two universes, two infinite beings which acted as unmoved movers, each in its own universe? Perhaps it was unthinkable. The word "universe" appeared to entail unity. "Universe" could only mean the sum total of what exists in space and time. How could there be more than one universe?

The professor remembered that some physicists had put it forward that there might be more than one universe, and that the laws of different universes might have nothing in common. In another universe there might be more truth-values open to propositions than simply truth on the one hand, and falsehood on the other. There could be a universe where sentences could be both true and false at the same time, where things might both exist and not exist at the same time, where a being might be both finite and infinite. Where, for example, the unmoved mover might be both present and absent. Such a universe would be indeed perplexing to live in. He wondered if he were not perhaps in fact living in such a universe, and not in the one he'd always imagined himself in, where contradictions excluded one another, where God either existed or He didn't, and no nonsense about it.

Sam the short-order man took hold of the professor's wrist and felt for a pulse. It was there, but much slowed.

"He's gone into a state of suspended animation," said Sam, in a tone of extreme annoyance. "No, really now, this has got to stop."

How could Sam tell that the professor had just taken an extreme metaphysical step, that of denying the possibility of there being more than one universe. As he did this, his pulse slowed to practically nothing; his body temperature dropped below 95; his respiration grew deep and slow and his eyeballs rolled way back into his head. Now he stopped thinking and began to imagine.

At first it seemed to him that he was standing in the middle of the sky, unsupported in any way. Yet he had no inclination to fall. He was simply at a point, with nothing around him. He couldn't see his arms or legs, and had no sensation of possessing a body, but he was at a point which he would describe as "there." He was located and he could move.

To move he simply thought about changing the point where he was, but it wasn't like floating around at all, as you might in a science-fiction movie. It was more like passing through a whole series of intervening there-points without moving in space, like a series of projected slides. No, not like that. Like a series of completely unconnected states of existing. Hard to express.

No sensation of strain or using the muscles, but he hadn't become an angel or anything like that. He was human, and what's more he was himself, though he had no name. But he was himself, and completely himself, not a baby. This wasn't a womb. Not dark.

It wasn't light either—there didn't seem to be any darkness or light or the intervening shades. The closest he could come to describing where he was might be to say that it was all a pale silver-grey, but it would be wrong to say that. He thought of colourlessness as a pale silver grey but of course it wasn't that at all. Not at all. He began to imagine he'd arrived at an unconditioned state of pre-existence where he was in his cause, that is, in or annexed to or issuing from or conceived by or held in the Divine Mind, in a state of unmixed creaturehood before locality caught him. Not before birth. More like in the idea of himself in the Creator's eternal contemplation of His Essence.

This was colourless but not invisible or outside the possibility of experience. It was not an annihilation of himself. It was like finally grasping the definition of himself, seeing everything he meant, unconditionally and in an instant.

Outside students came and went, expecting the professor to hand back their papers, neatly graded, but he never did. He wasn't dead, not what you'd call dead precisely. But a lot of people came to somebody's funeral.

Dark Glasses

This story comes from the quality of the light. I don't know why I went to the party wearing my clip-ons. The mid-February afternoon had featured strong sun-glare over snow, a hard-edged Northern Lights dazzle, and I'd needed the protection of the smoked lenses or imagined I had, which amounts to the same thing.

I don't think I had them on during dinner. I don't wear them around the house. To tell the truth, I feel pretty ambiguous about wearing dark glasses at any time, having read somewhere that hiding behind them is considered by psychiatrists to be a hostile act, which makes the person you're talking to uneasy and suspicious. Psychiatrists don't say what the content of the situation is when both parties are wearing dark glasses, but then psychiatrists are full of baloney anyway, so maybe I shouldn't worry about it.

Anyway I was due at the party in the middle of the evening, and somehow or other between dinner and my departure in the car I clipped the dark lenses onto my ordinary glasses. Thinking back I can remember feeling irritated that I'd likely spend the whole night taking them off to talk to people I liked, then putting them back on to conceal my eyes from other people. These clip-ons are light and cheap, not very good ones, with a thin nose-piece, which I've got in the habit of rolling between the thumb and forefinger of my left hand, flipping the Polaroid eyepieces back and forth, back and forth. My life is full of similar compulsive acts. Madness lies in wait all round.

And desperation. Driving east I rolled through seas of melting slush; the blackness of the night comforted me. I liked seeing the cityscape through manufactured opaqueness. I liked the swimming deception, disguising the way things were, and the impression that I was doing my vision some ghastly harm so that colour-blindness or worse would result. Night darker than night: only a dummy wears sunglasses at night, but I was wearing mine.

I climbed round and round, rising up through the dignities of Westmount to an idle street that ran nowhere, ending after six houses, all big, all bogus: half-timbering and plaster applied over brick, coats of arms carved in shoddy veneer. I parked as close as I could to the last house. Inside was a hall with two suits of armour, one here, one there, making the damn place look like the old Stoodleigh Restaurant under the Toronto *Star* building, something worked up by a decorator much attached to crown and empire. There were more coats of arms, these coloured, on the ceiling of the hall, two storeys above. A timbered staircase mounted grandly, first left, then right, to a gallery running along the south wall at the second-floor level. I don't suppose there really were lances and pennons, stuffed warhorses and arquebuses hanging above the gallery, but that's how I recollect the place, and the image establishes the tone. There were two barmen, hired for the night, and two waiters, and a girl checking coats. The house was big but not all *that* big.

I heard somebody saying, "He's a better writer than you," and somebody else saying, "You lie in your black throat," and heard an offer of bodily prostitution and the offer rejected, but I didn't pay too much attention. Later, I thought, later. It was going to be an evening devoted to the public life of politics and affairs and institutional art, to intrigue among persons seeking to have their writing published, and avowals of liberal and even radical social ethics on all sides. Men stated their solidarity with the Soledad brothers, ladies analyzed the influence of Marcuse on Miss Davis; nonsense was talked. I had trouble

120

finding a bottle of bitter lemon; people kept offering me champagne. This made me feel guilty of all the hemmed-in, sterile aspects of abstinence.

The big bar lay toward the pantry, where there was a lineup. It was a party to pay off many social debts in a single bound, the best sort of party for all concerned: for the giver because he needn't give another for three years, for the guests because their host's guilt feelings have impelled him to a demonstrative and clearly unnecessary abundance of provision.

All smoked. None smoked anything but tobacco. A party for the over-thirties and forties, with whom I feel the solidarity I cannot extend to the Soledad brothers. If there is such a thing as party spirit, it can validly be shared, I think, only with one's own age-group. It's chronology after all that fixes our allegiances. When I saw Herman Leventhal in the drawing-room, his wife at his elbow as always in a touching show of supportive affection, I felt like a son to him; this is because I'm fifteen years younger than he is, just too many years to feel like a brother though not quite enough in fact to be his son. Where does the generation gap start to show—at fifteen years? There is no generation gap; chronology flows unbroken. What I felt for Herman Leventhal is not the hostility the younger generation is supposed to feel for its elders but admiration and sorrow. Even in this place I might have removed my concealing dark slices of thin plastic for him, if only there hadn't been those others.

I made my way through dense crowds toward Mr. Leventhal until a man stopped me.

"I read a story of yours recently." He gave me the title.

"Oh, yes."

"It's a very sad story, isn't it?"

"All my stories are sad."

"Why is that?"

"How the hell should I know?" I said savagely. "Maybe I can only recognize sad stories. Some people are crippled like that and can only see disfigurement; we smell out hurt the way a dog traces his quarry. Most days I feel fairly good, but I'm always on the alert for others' misgivings. What else would you like to know?"

"Oh, that'll do." He said this so expressively that I laughed, then he laughed, feeling better. He couldn't see my eyes and I pushed rudely past. I don't often enjoy the luxury of rudeness. To be rude you have to be far far more heavily armoured than I am. This fellow might have punched me, but he was in a crowd and couldn't work his arms free. I felt I could afford to be direct. After I got by him I worked into a clearing in the jungle, a round gap in the mob six feet across. I took a deep breath and looked across the empty space at Herman and Yetta Leventhal, since this last winter more than ever together. She is a stocky woman with smooth grey hair parted on the side and worn with bangs in front. She has the composed face of a person of great capacity, and won't speak to you until she knows something about you, sometimes not then.

I first met Herman Leventhal when I agreed to act as an expert witness in an obscenity trial. That sounds funny. However, I'm not claiming to be an expert in the production of obscenity but only in its detection. I know smut when I see it, and I considered the book on trial as mighty high-class smut, so confoundedly literary as not to stimulate me, which has to be the test, doesn't it? The story of a great big zero. How does a pretentious piece of sentence-making, replete with nineteenth-century descriptions of moons racing through blackened skies, get a reputation as corrupting smut? Feeble, it was, feeble. Nobody was ever stimulated by such a book, or if they were they must have been in perpetual riot of stimulation from pantie-hose advertisements and deodorant commercials.

Actually I met Mr. Leventhal some time before the trial began, in his office on top of a downtown office block, so high that I shook with terror the whole time I was up there. The parapet or wall was low and the glass, who knows about it? I remember a horror story about a young executive talking on the phone on the 30th floor of such a building; he says to his caller, "Nonsense, the glasswall is perfectly safe," and kicks the panel of glass next to his desk. It falls out, shattering 300 feet below. Contracts, desk-blotter, note-pad, all are sucked through the window. A secretary saves herself by the strength of her grasp on a desk-leg. The young executive pees in his pants. I wasn't crazy about this law office, but in the interests of justice and civil liberty I went to a meeting there with three other smut-smellers. Three of us were allegedly qualified to take the stand on grounds of academic or other appointments, or because of work published. The fourth stammered when questioned.

"And of course, sir, as a lawyer, you see, I have no expert knowledge of the field, which is why I've invited you gentlemen today. Everyone knows Mr. A, I think, and Mr. B. Their status is fixed, and Mr. C is on the faculty of a distinguished institution. You, sir, I must say at once, I don't know. I think we should be frank from the beginning. Can you tell me why I might have been given your name?"

"I've written many of them," said Mr. D.

"Many what?"

"Obscene books."

This declaration was made wholly without shame.

Mr. Leventhal, heir to a sternly legal moral code, and its transmitter to the next generation, was of two minds about this reply.

"Will you clarify that for us?"

So Mr. D furnished a lot of clarification. "I started as a youngster in Paris, when I wrote the famous obscene third part of *Don Quixote* for a publisher whose name was a household word."

"Why was that?"

"Well, he was always on trial, the same thing as here."

"But here it's the bookseller who's been charged. Tell us,

123

Mr. D, what do you think of that, bringing charges against the utterer, so to speak, of smut, if it is smut?"

"Indefensible. Look at Denmark and Sweden!"

Mr. Leventhal didn't undermine this breach of the forms of legal reasoning. All he said was, "What is legal in Scandinavia isn't necessarily legal here. The question is not what ought to be allowed, but what is in fact allowed by our enactments. I must say, Mr. D, that I would consider it an error of tactics to employ you as a defence witness in this proceeding, and I will not do so. But I will rely on you throughout for expert advice. Can you tell me, for example, what the returns are from a reputedly obscene work?"

"It's just like any other literary work," said the author pettishly, "it depends on your publisher and the publicity. A really good dirty book may often be overlooked in favour of one that isn't nearly so good."

"What is the standard?"

"Of merit?"

"First of merit, then of dirt."

Here Mr. D was at a loss. "About merit—if you mean merit as literature—I'm unable to speak. As for how dirty the book is, I think the test must be what it causes you to do." He was about to embroider this view with a wealth of detail when Mr. Leventhal tactfully dismissed him. I note that this is the same view I hold myself and freely advance, though I must state here that I haven't hidden myself behind the initial D. In the recital just concluded, as a matter of fact, I figure unostentatiously as poor Mr. C.

That's how I got to know Herman and Yetta, through attending that meeting and sitting around for days on end outside courtrooms waiting for proceedings, which once under way dragged on interminably, to begin. Like me, justice moves slowly and wears dark glasses.

I learned during those long waits that the Leventhals were famous activists in the vanguard of the civil-liberties movement. In deportation proceedings against socialist seamen, Herman would be valiantly and constantly opposed to the Immigration Department. Trade unionism found in him an ardent counsel. He has fought all his life against all forms of censorship and thought-control: rules against the importation of certain books, harassment of small presses, obscenity proceedings, closings of sexy movies. Such things go on all the time. Book are seized at borders daily. Draft-dodgers, so-called, are illegally detained and bunted into the outstretched arms of their pursuers. This happens. It shouldn't but it does.

Herman and Yetta have hungered and thirsted after justice since the early nineteen-thirties. Strikebreaking proceedings against Oshawa auto-workers begun by an infamous government of the most illiberal tendency were their first battleground. Asbestos caused them a second long stand at the barricades. Lady Chatterley leaned on them for deliverance and got it, in the end. They can't be praised enough for courage, for persistence in the face of adversity. Of course I had no way of knowing that when I was sitting, teeth chattering, in that dizzying office, hoping that the walls wouldn't fall off—they looked awfully transparent.

If things are to be built of glass, let it be dark glass that confers an illusory solidity. I stood looking across blank space at Herman and Yetta, remembering what I'd heard about them over the winter. Their only son, Chaim, had died suddenly. I couldn't recall what he had died of; it's a question I never ask when I hear. I keep my horrified questions to myself. What could it have been. Heart? Cancer? Cancer of what? I don't want to know.

Herman said, "We've been wanting to see you." I started to tremble and grow sensitive to the strange modes of light moving in the room. Have you ever been in a dimly lit drawing-room full of rejoicing, drinking artists and writers and their hubbub, and seen what light there was draw in and around the magnified figure of a single person? That's how it was. Herman was wearing a handsome blue suit. If it didn't seem insulting I'd describe him as impeccably tailored. He used to favour dark blue and grey suits that fitted him beautifully; he had stayed thin well into his fifties. His hair is such a smooth, full, close-cropped grey that it's nearly blue, silver-blue. If you were trying to imagine a distinguished civil libertarian who was lean, handsome and aging gracefully, you would imagine Herman Leventhal. Blue and silver and fine chalk pinstripe, neat moustache, penetrating eyes and this absurd halo around him of—I can see I won't get this across—of dark light.

If you ask me how light can be dark, I can't say, but that was exactly how it was. Let me see if I can explain the phenomenon. My smoked lenses may have had something to do with it. You might simply exclaim, "Take them off, stupid, and the effect will go away," but that wouldn't be right, as the event showed. The room was dark enough, and there was a big fire in a fireplace of walk-in dimensions. Firelight in February is apt to induce romantic illusions, as every Canadian knows, but it wasn't simply the firelight or the dark glasses, or the heavy floor lamp over behind Yetta, with its fringe of bobbles. The way they kept looking at me made me feel that I'd risen from the dead without first having died, a dreadful feeling.

"You youngsters never grasp the principles of true socialism, never see how national aspirations may justly be annexed to them; you believe that every time such a program is tried it transforms itself at once into Nazism, but you're wrong. Give national feeling a chance, why won't you?"

I said, "Herman, it's me."

Yetta moved closer to him, taking his right arm and shoulder in a tight grasp. "We learned in a bitter school," she said grimly; "we were in Palestine in '38, you know. You think because you've heard of the Balfour Declaration that you know all about international Zionism and its history. But Herman was invoking the principles of the Hague Convention to free boys on the border of Jordan while you were still dirtying your diapers. You find in textbooks that socialism and the political identity of Israel don't match together very well, and you remember the paradox of National Socialism under Hitler, and you conclude that what we've fought for is self-defeating and self-contradictory. But I say that the impulse to achieve social justice expressible in any post-Marxist analysis of politics or economics, though it may express itself in internationalist terms—the unattainable paradise of the international socialist brotherhood—will root itself in a state, whether Québec, Israel or the thousand-year Reich."

"Right," said Herman, shaking his arm back and forth in her grip.

I wondered if I was having an hallucination, or if maybe they had jointly taken leave of their senses, so I put my hands slowly to my earpieces, took my glasses off, removed the clip-ons and polished the clear lenses, afterward putting my glasses back on and holding the clip-ons between thumb and forefinger. I started that compulsive flipping, back and forth. Now and then Yetta and Herman glanced first at my hand, then at each other.

With my clarified vision I recognized that the dark light that had so surprised me as it formed around this troubled couple was now if anything intensified. What was it? Where did this alien shadow originate? Herman came close to me, as if about to seize me by the lapel, but I had no lapel, just a sweater. Perhaps my clothes had an unjustifiably youthful air that misled him. I'm 43 years old and never wear a suit, just sweaters and pants. That must have been it; there was nothing for him to get hold of. He obviously had me mixed up with somebody else.

"I don't know the whole story of socialism or nationalism," I said, "but I'm willing to learn, I really am. Why don't you tell me what you think?" I moved closer to them, working our little group in under a looming shadow, against a corner wall. "How can nationalist feeling work with socialist brotherhood?

I can't see how that could happen."

"That's because you don't know anything. Why do you think Marx marked out the Russian proletariat as the inheritors of the traditional Messianic role of the Jewish people? Eh, why?"

"Well, actually, I don't know."

"He admits he doesn't know."

"It's a concession," said Yetta.

Herman said, "Marx was devoted to the suffering and the dying. He wouldn't recognize in the prosperous, bourgeois German Jew a potential saviour. But your Russian proletarian, Jew or Gentile, ah, there was the insulted and injured man, the sufferer who would redeem the world. It was in the tragic history of the weakening Russian regime, not in the German or the American, certainly not in the so-well-satisfied-with-itself British political system, that he discovered the dwelling-place of political man-as-such. Historical movements never begin in the world at large: they must be rooted in a place or they are nothing. The Papacy, with its paradoxical Roman universalism, knew this well enough. You Canadians. . ."

"You're a Canadian," I said ardently, and Yetta spit at me like a cat. "Look," I said, "I was awfully sorry to hear about Chaim. If I could say. . ."

"Chaim, Chaim, what is that?" Herman said, making a brushing motion with his left hand. "The error of the activist is to invoke the strike weapon too readily. The strike is like the peace officer's weapon; it must exist but should never be used, and the union leader who pulls men off the job has taken from them something that can never be replaced, a day's productivity. The artist never goes on strike; he can't afford to lose one day, one hour. Let us assume a typical working year of 250 days, multiplied by the 45 years of a working lifetime, this gives you 11,250 days in a man's working life. Every day lost is gone forever, can never be replaced. The union leader may think that an increase in wages or a betterment in working conditions will compensate for time lost, but it never can, it never can. You cannot call back time lost."

I now had the impression that Chaim's ghost was standing in front of me. I seemed to be turning into him. "We have no quarrel with the young," said Yetta, her face twisted grotesquely, "we only want to explain certain facts. Let Herman tell you how things really are. He knows."

"I'm ready to be told, I'm listening, say whatever you like."

"No," he said, "no, you won't listen, you don't let me tell you. I can't reach you."

I looked at them appalled; they seemed shrunken, huddled together and feeble. I clipped the dark lenses onto my glasses again and put them over my eyes, wishing they would do the same. I wanted their faces covered up. I could not bear the sight of them.

An Allegory of Man's Fate

Bronson kept seeing them tacking back and forth, sometimes in pairs, occasionally in squadrons, on the blue surface of the lake. The pretty scene moved him obscurely—roused some atavistic, long-repressed need for space, sun, shimmer off the water, silence. In the early autumn he bought a kit, intending to attempt to assemble the boat in his basement—conveniently large—in the city over the winter. In mid-October, just after the family had returned from an exceptionally fine Thanksgiving weekend at the cottage, a very large red truck appeared in front of the house about five o'clock in the afternoon, disruptive of the cocktail hour and dinner. There were two cumbersome, terribly heavy, cardboard cartons to be wrestled off the truck and into the recreation room. They would not go through the side door because of the angle; the driver and his helper were inclined to bugger off at once. They wanted their evening meal, like anybody else. It was only by giving them $5 apiece that Viv Bronson, who looked awfully pretty with her cheeks flushed in annoyance, persuaded them to hang around and shift this heavy weight or that, up on one end, on its side, on the other end, around this way. Back. Crash; tinkle. Oh oh.

"They won't go in that way."

"No."

"What's in these, missus?"

"A boat. The parts for a boat."

"Parts only?" The implication was clear to Bronson who now hove into view—the nautical expression seems appropriate—behind the delivery men.

"Won't it go down?" he asked, and the others turned to gaze at him.

"No."

"Have you tried it up on end?"

"Yes."

"Have you tried it on its side?"

"Yes."

"We gotta go now, sir, Missus. Gotta go, yes, the truck is out on a lease basis, see? The boss don't own the truck, just leases it on a lease basis from nine to six, eh? Has to be back in the yard by six or goes on the overtime rate. We're going now, goodbye now." Off they went, leaving Mr. and Mrs. Bronson standing beside the long, heavy, wide carton jammed in the side entryway. The other, longer, thinner, not quite so heavy, rattling carton lay in the driveway in puddles of overnight rain, cardboard going soggy, Bronson saw. Both cartons were bound by metal stripping with viciously sharp ends and edges.

"Where are the kids?"

"How should I know? Where are they ever? Probably down the Azlex shoplifting."

"No need to fuss."

"... not fussing..."

"We'll try through the front hall then." He found rising to his lips an observation he had never needed to record in his tranquil life until then, and said without thinking, for the first time. "There is no difficulty that cannot be overcome." His wife nodded. Feeling an enriched married mutual understanding, they first lifted the longer, now melting carton from the puddles and bore it, afraid that their hands would punch holes in the sodden cardboard, along the driveway to the front of the house, up the stairs onto the verandah.

Mrs. Fletcher next door happening to emerge from her home that moment, looking for the *Star* carrier, as usual very late, looked startled when she saw them.

"Somebody's getting a new mattress," she called.

"It's the spars," said Mrs. Bronson through her teeth.

"What, dear?"

"It's the *spars*."

"Aha. Aha. The *Star*."

They let the carton down carefully and began to pull it through the door.

"Have you had your *Star* yet?"

They got the box into the hall, where it filled the space at the foot of the stairs. Bronson now began to wonder whether the thing would go down the cellar staircase and into the rec room. He saw that a command decision would be involved and tried to think ahead. From the verandah, Mrs. Fletcher called in through the doorway, "Have you had your *Star*?"

"No, spars. The *spars*."

"No, have you had your *Star*? Has the boy been by?"

"Oh. No. Well, actually we don't take from the carrier boy any more. I just go over to the corner before dinner. I should go soon before he closes. Would you like me to get you a paper, uh, Alice?"

He never felt easy about calling the neighbours by their Christian names.

"No," she said, after deliberatiion. "I'll chance it. He's almost always late."

Bronson said to his wife, "Going for the paper, Viv."

"What, and leave this great thing here? And what about the one stuck in the side door?"

"I'll get it when I come back. Only be five minutes, darling."

Walking to the neighbourhood variety store, he felt doubt gathering in his mind. If he took the two huge objects downstairs as they stood, this would give him a rough idea whether or not he could get the assembled boat out again when the time came. This was clearly a paramount matter, requiring immediate clarification. The finished boat might very well prove bulkier than the boxes, probably would. The phrase "eleven feet long overall" came to mind, recollected from the newspaper advertisement that had incited the purchase. How wide? If a dinghy was eleven feet long, about how wide would it be? He found himself passing through Joe's doorway. He bought the paper and a Doctor West nylon-bristled medium hard, as a wedge for the conversation. "You live over the store, right?" he said to Joe, the owner.

"Yeah, correct, why?"

"Doing anything tonight?"

Joe's face slowly acquired a threatened expression; this was the first time in over seven years that Bronson had ever said anything to him apart from requests for this or that article— razorblades, paperbacks. He said, "What were you thinking of?"

"Involves heavy lifting."

Joe moved away from the counter, spreading his suitcoat open, plucking at his shirttail. For an hallucinated instant, Bronson thought he was going for a gun. "This is it," he told himself. Actually the storekeeper was opening his trousers. "See?" he said.

"What?"

"Triple hernia," he announced with satisfaction.

That hard leather lump down there, Bronson realized, was some part of a truss. He felt relief. "I thought I'd ask," he said, picking up his change and his toothbrush. He looked at the toothbrush absently. "Maybe I'll have yellow instead," he said.

"Take your pick. . . or there's the Py-Co-Pay line with the rubber tip, at the same price."

"Got what I want."

He folded the paper into a tight flat package and strolled back to the house, where Vivianne had dinner already on the table. "You want a sherry, or do you want to go ahead?" she said.

"Let's eat."

They sat through the meal in silence, oppressed by sober reflection. Though the weekend weather had been idyllic, it had rained on Tuesday. Now it was cooling. From time to time the aluminum side door creaked in the freshening breeze and gusts of air chilled Bronson's ankles. Once he almost got up to go and shut the side door, then remembered that it was propped open by his purchase. He sneaked a peek at Viv, at the other end of the table; she held a lamb chop in her fingers, nibbling delicately, close to the bone, a pink crinkled pantie dangling insecurely from the gnawed end. She smiled at him over the chop.

She said, "It'll be all right."

Later in the evening they were able to work the tall narrow box of spars into a permanent standing position, on end in the staircase well, such that one end extended upward almost to the second floor, like the brass pole in a fire hall. Bronson stood at the foot of the stairs, looking up and estimating how the mast would look when stepped in place. It would be tall and straight. He imagined a gentle swell, deck lifting under him, conversational water.

"There's the other one," said Viv breathlessly.

It was harder to extricate the heavier carton from the frame of the side entry, where it had caught on the hinges and the hook for the latch; there was breakage; the carton was punctured here and there; from its interior came disquieting sounds of shifting bits of heavy stuff, each time they moved it. But there was no way—it had to come out and back and along the driveway and up and inside when, exhausted, arm muscles aching, Bronson and his wife began to quarrel and insult one another. It was in the middle of a pitched battle that their teen-aged children, boy and girl, arrived home from different ends of the city.

"You're a feeble fool!"

"And you're living on the earnings of a feeble fool. So take care!"

"I should say. I should say."

"So you should."

"I will, then."

"See that you do!"

"What is all this?" said their daughter, Irene, sticking her head in the door. Behind her, Gary, fifteen, heavily moustached, sideburned, leather-jacketed, could be heard demanding, "Is it safe to bring my mandolin in? Or will they wreck it?"

Bronson had once smashed a valuable antique, a blue crystal pitcher, in a fit of rage, shouting out that the spout was wretchedly designed and slopped over. Gary, sitting next to him at table, had been powerfully impressed by the violent action, never forgot it, and used to keep wooden, fragile things out of his father's way. From long witness of silent movies and cartoons on children's TV, he had gotten quite used to the idea of smashing ukuleles and mandolins over people's heads— this happened all the time on the little screen. He could imagine his father, in the grip of impulse, grabbing his cherished mandolin and lowering it on Mother's pate with disastrous effect.

Vivianne started to laugh weakly. "Yes. No. It's this boat of your father's."

"It's for all of us," Bronson said. "We'll all have fun building it, and then sailing it." Afterward he wondered if this speech had exhibited the savage, unknowing pride of strength and power called *hubris* by the Greeks—an attitude that delivers punishment in its very structure. He got to his feet, made room for Gary to enter, and invited his son to help him store the second carton; they decided in the end to slide it in behind a breakfront buffet which stood in the dining-room and almost concealed the box. It stayed there the whole winter. The family decided after long consultation not to open the boxes and build the boat downstairs.

"That would make the basement unuseable for any other purpose all winter and maybe longer," said Irene sagely, and all agreed.

"We'll build it at the lake," said Bronson. "We'll carry it out right in the cartons; no need to mess with it here."

By Christmas he had stopped thinking about his boat as such, as boat-in-being. Instead the form of the tall narrow carton of spars grew in his mind, taking various shapes and traces of suggestion as he imagined it from time to time: as scaffold in western film, as totem pole. Finally it assumed and retained the dark vague shape of a grandfather clock, perhaps because of the dim light lying along the stairwell, coming in the end to embody in Bronson's imagination the powers of ancient law.

In spring wide-flung doors dissipated this dimness; curtains around the window on the landing were drawn well back, admitting pale sunlight and good air. With May Day at hand, the family rented a U-Haul for their annual first weekend at the lake, loaded it with mattresses, extra oddments of cottage furniture and, this year, uniquely, their potential boat. The drive out—by no means a short distance—was accomplished with surprising ease, the cottage fittings carried conveniently into the cedar-smelling small building. Then with gratifying rapidity the four of them hustled the two cartons onto the sundeck overlooking the shore, set up a pair of sawhorses presumed to be essential to the construction project, then stood back and gazed fearfully at the never-yet-opened, battered holed objects. They had certainly managed to take on a heavy charge of *mana*, Bronson conceded, a load of family spirits and folk narratives that dwelt on and in them. To open them would be a very serious business. That weekend they recoiled; they covered the tabernacle with tarpaulin and returned to town to meditate.

The actual unveiling took place much later. They had hoped to get up over the twenty-fourth, but this proved impossible. June was dissipated on a business trip Bronson had to take, an annual affair. This time he asked Viv to go with him, an unprecedented request, possibly with concealed motive, and they spent a happy two weeks in and around Toronto. No boat-building got done that month.

On Canada Day weekend, Bronson steeled himself to cut. He sent Gary and Irene off to the landing with their pals for the day, then persuaded Viv to stand and watch as he tore the end off the big box, the one with the parts for the hull inside. He slid out many—many—long sheets of marine plywood. Bottles of starter fluid. Cans of glue powder. Strips of mahogany. Long strips of ash. Spindles and cutouts and plugs and blocks. "Good wood in this anyhow," he said, panting.

There was a clear plastic sack of white ropes.

There was a second clear plastic sack of brown ropes.

And another one full of strong, slender wire cables and rings and shackles.

There were many tiny clear plastic bags of different-sized nails.

And screws.

There were the sails, mainsail and jib, beautiful orange-red nylon with the sailmaker's logo in their corners.

"Red sails," said Viv, pleased, "how lovely."

Bronson didn't answer. He had found a pair of instruction manuals deep in the recesses of this carton, one on sailing, one on assembly. He forebore to open them, instead lining up the legions of parts, fitments, forms, indisputable shapes, on the sundeck. He upended the ragged carton and shook it for several seconds. A tiny square-headed copper nail fell out. He had a terrible fear that if he threw out the carton he would accidentally dispose of some essential irreplaceable piece, lodged in one of the folded ends. He carried the cardboard tenderly in his extended arms around to the flat, sun-drenched rocks behind the building, where he proceeded to tear it into little squares, with convulsive energy, removing first the flaps, then the sides. Every morsel of cardboard was haken vigorously, as Viv stood by watching with anxiety. In the end, he was satisfied. No fugitive nail would lose this battle.

There was the second, or long and thin, carton to be gutted. This proved a simple matter, as only the mast, the gaff, the boom, and the oars were involved. These handsome, already half-shaped and dressed, wooden pieces slid neatly along the rafters of cottage interior until they were required, an age to come, while along the floor of the sundeck lay the other bits of boat. Hundreds and hundreds of them. I never thought it would be like this, he told himself, an exceeding great multitude. Behind him, plucking repeatedly at her lips with one hand and holding a manual open in the other, his wife checked through a complex list.

"They're numbered," she said slowly. "Every piece is stamped somewhere and if two or more bits serve the same purpose, they've got the corresponding number."

"I guess what we ought to do now," he said, working it out as he spoke, "is check over the list and make sure we've got everything." He could feel rationality reviving in himself, like an engine warming on a cold day, and was comforted. As Viv read off the list, he scrambled around on his knees, locating the objects numbered and so oddly named. At first things were easy, early numbers referring to the great sheets of lusciously grained plywood which would in the end form the boat's hull. Of these there were more than a dozen, none more than eight feet long. Bronson wondered how the boat could possibly be eleven feet long, if no piece extended so far, and was speedily enlightened. These extensive sheets were grouped together and stacked against the front wall of the cottage, where they remained until actual construction began.

"What the hell is this?" Bronson demanded at large, holding up a long, silky, ravelling roll of pale silvery tape.

"Appears to be fibreglass," said his wife, in her W. C. Fields voice, as she bent her gaze on the manual. Eventually they figured out what it was for.

"Don't you dig things out and ask me," she complained,

"let's go along by the numbers."

"Yeah, yeah, what the hell is this?" He held up a metal object in light alloy, of decidedly suggestive shape. His wife blushed. "It's an upper pintle."

"So you say."

"But it is. It is. Come on, sweetie, let me call them out."

"Oh all right."

"Looking for number 47. 'Boom-kicking-strap-chock,' " she chanted.

"What is that? I don't even know what I'm looking for. What would that look like?"

"Don't know."

" 'Boom-kicking-strap-chock'?"

"That's what it says. Number 47."

It was a little cube of hardwood, no bigger than an Oxo cube. "What can it be?" marvelled Bronson. "What can it do?"

"Number 79. 'After-deck-batten-support.' "

"Is there only one?"

"One only, correct."

"Got it."

"Number 80. 'Quarter knees.' "

"How many?"

"Two of these, I think, yes, two."

"What would they look like?"

"It says they're mahogany, would this be them? Yes, here they are."

"All right, Viv, you read the book, I'll find the pieces. Okay? These are hard like rock."

"Number 83." She paused, staring at the text in alarm.

"What is it?"

" 'Plate-case-packing-pieces.' "

The total opacity of this phrase excited paroxysms of horror and despair, and they took off for the rest of the day. Dinner at the landing with multiple drinks partially restored their spirits; the next day they persevered, finished checking their list, and read off a little surprise note at the back of the manual which informed them that their tool kit was wholly inadequate for the task impending. They drove at once to the nearest hardware store and bought Surform tools in various shapes, a large, solid, hand plane, an electric drill, an electric sander, drill bits in many sizes. Finally they owned everything necessary.

"And after, we'll have them," said Bronson.

Construction now began; they learned straightaway how an eleven-foot boat materializes from eight-foot pieces of ply. Butt-strapping! Now I know what butt-strapping is, Bronson thought, something learned, new valuable experience, never to be forgotten. I am enlarging my range, confronting and overcoming obstacles; nothing human is alien to me. Without realizing that he spoke aloud, he said, "There is no difficulty that cannot be overcome." His wife, sitting down hard on a glued butt-strap join, now drying, twisted round and stared at him.

"Don't move for a minute," he said, "it's almost dry."

"Now for the nails."

"It says to back up anything you're driving nails in by something solid like a piece of iron or block of hardwood. I wonder what it means."

Viv said, " It means if you don't you'll nail your piece of wood to the floor."

"Ha ha, very funny." All the same, he dug out a kiln-dried beam-end left over from construction of the cottage and used it as a back-up. Kneeling on the ply, feeling the solidity of this support and noting that the wood didn't bounce and recoil under hammer blows, he understood the instructions, and said to his wife, "When I read it in the book, I didn't understand, but after I'd done it, I could see."

Life continued. When the long hull forms had been glued, trimmed, nailed, hundreds of small holes had to be drilled along their sides to allow them to be *sewn together* with copper wire. This seemed a simple task, but after cutting 250 wire bits,

Viv found that the tip of her thumb and forefinger on her right hand were abraded, blistered, then cut and bleeding; it was the bright end of each shard of wire, coming away from the snips, that kept nibbling the fleshy tips. She sucked them and stared resentfully at Bronson, busy drilling holes along the hull form edges. "You took the easy job," she said.

He lifted his head and wiped dripping sweat from his eyes. "Gives you the hell of a stiff neck, this does. Want to have a go?"

She had second thoughts.

In a day or two they laid the plywood sheets on top of the sawhorses and started to lace them up tight with the lengths of wire, twisting and knotting them with pliers. This proved a relatively easy matter to begin with, growing harder the closer the edges came together; there was the artistic problem of forming the chine of the hull, as the later bits of wire drew in tight. The plywood edges were nipped in hard against each other; one person had to mold the desired form into the wood by main force, while the other threaded the cutting and irritating wires through tiny holes. At the end of the week they had four sore thumbs and four lacerated forefingers. And the formed hull standing bravely on the sawhorses. They shot a roll of film of themselves standing beside it, patting it.

Then the really hard part started.

Bronson said later on that the deception involved in the proceeding was that you had something looking like a completed boat very early, but it took months—possibly years—to finish it off. He considered this a rude parody of the conditions of human existence. They had to learn how to handle the liquid resin and strips of fibreglass that sealed tight the boat's sewn seams. This involved timing the hardening process of the resin, a stinking, poisonously blue goo. The first few times they did it, it snapped solid, BANG, like the lid of a closing trunk, before they had time to use it. Then it refused to harden because they didn't put in enough hardener. Then they got it timed right for a hot dry day and the weather turned cold and damp, throwing them off; paranoia threatened, but they learned, they learned. They got so much fibreglass on the hull they had to write to the city for more.

Virtually nothing was simple. They found that the sun beat down on them fiercely in the later part of the day, but they had so much junk stacked on the deck that there could be no question of moving to a shadier place. From time to time they broke small pieces. Bronson learned to improvise. "It's all educational. There is no difficulty. . ." His wife and children cursed under their breath and he let the remark trail off.

One day it took Bronson and Viv five desperate hours of sanding, smoothing, whittling, trimming, to get two small wooden pieces into place and securely glued. The further they went the closer the tolerances were, and the smaller the margin for error. Once they got a pleasant surprise. The deck tops, four imposing large pieces, fell into place as if they had been tailored to fit by master boatbuilders (of course they had). They grinned at each other, may even have exchanged kisses —their first in many days. Bronson thought: we will endure, we will go on to the end. They had managed every fitment but the last; only the inner and outer gunwales remained.

"Now for these we ought to have clamps," said Viv. "We're not strong enough in the hands to glue them, screw them and hold them against the hull by ourselves."

But Bronson had spent more than he could admit to himself on extra equipment, and now called a halt. "We'll do without," he said, and they were able to glue the outer gunwales into place by the unaided force of their thumbs. There were cracks where the fit wasn't dead flush, but on the whole the correct curve of the hull was followed. It was the inner gunwales that brought disaster. As they were trying to force the first of them to fit, there was a frighteningly loud crack. The piece snapped at the stress-point. The kit had come from Great Britain.

Bronson felt his eyes bug in his head. Minute points of light danced in them as he shut and opened his lids. He said, "There is no difficulty that cannot be overcome."

His wife said, "If you say that once more, at any time, I'll leave you."

He looked at her. He saw that she meant it.

"This afternoon if necessary."

"We've done enough for this summer," said Bronson. "I don't want to spoil everybody's vacation." His wife made no reply. They gathered up the fragments in silence, and put them away for the winter. The following spring, they were able to have a replacement gunwale shaped locally by hand. They bought a dozen large clamps. They fastened those last few pieces to the hull with loud and cheerful cries. Then they sanded it down and sanded it again and again. Fitted the rudder together. Screwed on oarlocks, pintles, eyes, varnished, varnished, sanded, painted, sanded, painted, painted, painted, painted... rigged. Hoisted their burgee.

The next summer, reaching and running on his blue lake, Bronson remembered nothing of what had passed.